Checking Out and Other Tales

Mary D'Arcy

The Fine Line
Edinburgh

The Fine Line
65 Lorne Street
Edinburgh
EH6 8QG
UK

ISBN: 978-1-908825-06-3

Praise for Mary D'Arcy's Work

"Bridgie and Mattie are endearing and fun. Great characters, with the potential for being the foundation for a lively comedy series." Stephen McCrum, BBC Producer/Script Editor, on Mary's sitcom pitch, Bagge & Baggage.

"Note well the name Mary D'Arcy. She totes a saucy pen and could become the funniest Ulster Poet of '86." Eddie McIlwaine, Belfast Telegraph on Terry Turkey: A Trilogy.

"Knuckling Under worked on a lot of levels for me. It told me a lot of different stories. The biting black humour really reminded me of a lot of my mother's work." Virginia Brownlow, on awarding Mary the 12th Molly Keane Creative Writing Award 2009.

"I wish my mother had lived long enough to hear this." Jimmy T Murakami, Filmmaker, Director of The Snowman and When the Wind Blows, on hearing Mary's pitch for Checking Out at the Galway Film Festival 2007.

"Although I have read your piece a dozen times I still get a wry chuckle from it. I imagine that any audience will do and so I am delighted that it will be the piece used on the last night of the play [Tea Chests and Dreams]." Dermot Bolger, April 2012 on Butter Pats and Climbing Roses.

"In her novel, Tale of Hoffman, Mary takes a funny and penetrating look at why a marriage falls apart." On being shortlisted for the Sitric Books Paperbackwriter Competition 2004.

To my husband - gentleman, scholar, muse - with love
and respect

Acknowledgements

Jimmy T Murakami, mentor and guru, in grateful thanks for his many trips to Belfast, his friendship, encouragement, belief in my work.

Erna Naughter, wife of the late Bill Naughton, in grateful thanks for her friendship, comments, and encouragement.

Kate Gould, writer, editor, publisher. Forgiven for coming after me with her literary shears, slashing what I thought was my best work, cutting and hacking until she "saw something in it", saying "Dandy" when *Tale of Hoffman* got its airing.

Gay Byrne who in the past broadcast my work and set Terry Turkey to music.

Pauline O'Hare, writer/author for all her advice and unfailing friendship.

Marie "Ma" McQuillan, Head of Drama at St Mary's College, who gave me my first writing assignment all those years ago.

Allen White, Australian sounding board/ researcher,who put me right about kookaburras.

Angela Kent, who bullies me into working on all those days the pen runs dry.

Bryan Sweeney BSc who gave me the kernel for *Checking Out.*

My offspring for bearing with me.

The friends I've been neglecting.

My mother, Tecie, for her neverending kindness and devotion.

And last but not least my best friend and long suffering husband for his forbearance, advice, wisdom and wit.

Fundamentally, all writing is about the same thing; it's about dying, about the brief flicker of time we have here, and the frustration that it creates.

Mordecai Richler

Contents

Introduction

Reading Mary D'Arcy's work, I am struck each time by the range and miscellany of the tales she tells. And not just stories and essays but screenplays, monologues, and comic verse - often biting, always emotive, and showing a keen grasp of human nature. One of her strengths is the knack she has of building up a minor character such as Sally in *Checking Out*, Selby in *You Are Dead*, or the midwife in *Here's to You, Mrs R* to hilarious effect. In the lean economy of her laconic prose she will raise up the underdog such as Paddy in *The Sub-Postmistress* in the same way she will bring down the supercilious such as the insufferable narrator in *Diary of a Lower Master*.

Striking, also, is the fact that she never allows herself to be swayed by the success of one publication into repeating a formula. Each story, each poem, each play is different to the one that went before. The situations can be anything from romantic love to black humour to comedy of manners, through to thrillers and the coldest and most shocking of crimes. All of which she will allude to as hard cold slices of life. Yet, almost every slice in her present collection is compelling enough to have picked up prizes, to be optioned by production companies, commissioned by myself/the Irish Film Board, and the BBC.

For one who uses the tool of language with such skill and ease, it is to be hoped she will carry on writing, and that this first anthology of her "shorts" will serve as a springboard to even greater literary success in the future.

Jimmy T Murakami

July 2012

Cry of the Kookaburra

There was nothing in her manner to alert him.

No stiffening of her posture.

No lingering gaze.

No quickly averted eye.

Yet every animal instinct he had was signalling wildly that she knew him.

Gillespie lay on the hospital bed and tried not to flinch as the stethoscope slid across his chest. A tsunami of pain ringed outwards from his ribs with every breath he drew. Yet her presence cured him as though his pain had been toothache and she a dentist. When, with a barely perceptible nod, she left him, pain resumed its sway.

Time passed - an hour, a day, a decade, a whole evolutionary era - yet the hands of his watch by some crazy illusion recorded this stretch of aeons as seventy seconds.

She doesn't know you. It isn't her.

It was the voice of reason, persuading him that trauma and conscience had conjured her up.

For a moment his terrors were laid to rest, and

the awareness that his wife would be with him shortly, did away with any lingering doubts.

"Hi."

A Chinese doctor materialised, and with unconscious arrogance, dealt him a shot, and after that a tiny beaker of something bitter.

Gillespie felt his body slacken. Pain ebbed.

It seemed like a new sensation, this sudden freedom from torment, and he spilt over like a brimming chalice of thankfulness.

Peace enfolded him.

His eyes closed, opened, closed again.

"Need you to sign this?"

It was a question that didn't expect an answer, and followed by a playful rap on the elbow.

Gillespie surfaced, and without opening his eyes, tried to monitor the voice.

"Not checking out on me, are you?"

Cajoling, smoke-cured by cigarettes, but Melbourne through-and-through. Although he willed it to be her, he knew it wasn't.

"You with us, Mr McGill?"

Gillespie opened his eyes.

An Aborigine stood in profile, patiently waiting to be noticed. One hand showed him a folder, the other a pen.

"I'm nurse Hollis." She smiled with a practised show of affability. "Consent form?"

Gazing at her snowy ballpoint pen, and the curve of the fingers that gripped it, something awoke in a cobwebby region of Gillespie's mind - something he didn't think should be disturbed. But whatever it was, it sighed, and went back to sleep again.

Gillespie looked up. Nurse Hollis was busy scribbling. About her hung whiffs of disinfectant, and he could smell whatever soap she had used to wash her hands.

He drew a shaky breath. "Could you tell me -"

"They're putting you under," she said, in a prosaic voice, and passed him a yellow form. "Broke yeh collar bone," she added cheerfully. "Yeh ribs -"

"What I mean -"

"Oh, the Berlingo?"

Gillespie closed his eyes in a gesture of patient endurance. Hollis didn't seem to notice. Using her pen to chase an itch behind her ear, she carried on in the weary tones of the traffic cop who has seen it all before, and knows he'll see it all again.

"Total write-off. Miracle you wasn't killed. You and yore passenger. You drivin' fast or what?"

"The doctor," he said, in a toneless voice and bringing his hand to his brow. "The lady examined me?"

"Huh?"

"Who was she?"

"Oh. The anaesthetist?" Hollis's mouth noticeably slackened, her eyes began to narrow. It was the face of someone trying to call up a telephone number. "That'd be…Dr Spellman?"

Spellman.

Relief flooded him.

Not her, then.

And how could it be? What would be the chances? Ten thousand miles and fifteen years removed from home -

"Yo?"

He took the pen, and signed his name - the one on his passport since '91.

"Thirty minutes, and thatchoo." Hollis gathered up her things and bustled across to the door. There she paused, and glared at him over her shoulder. "Pecker up, okay? Sun will shine feh you again."

From somewhere Gillespie trawled up a smile.

His gaze drifted to the window, grey with the grime of years. Smoke from a far off chimney looped sluggishly skywards. Above it a nimbus of gold cloud wrapped up the dying sun.

His eyelids drooped.

Tomorrow he'd watch the pink stains of sunset on the Dandenongs, and smile with Giancarla, remembering his terrors of the night before.

He dozed.

Strange thoughts shot through his brain, jumbled up with flickering drug-induced images: sheep shit littering the back of the van, a squaddy walking backwards, Jude Law thumbing a lift, flames licking up from an overturned bus, the cry of the kookaburra *don't do it, don't do it*, Law's hand hugging his thigh, the view from the Crumlin Road jail, a slick of oil on a dusty road, ebony fingers snowy pen frangipanis rushing towards him -

Whoomp.

Gillespie's eyelids opened.

Through them he blinked at the figure silhouetted against the window. Crouched, white-coated, biding its time -

But no. His eyes opened wider. Nobody there.

Only the curtain billowing in.

Fear receded.

Mists closed down on his brain once again, and Belfast, the figure, the backpacker, Melbourne, all floated off into unfathomable distances, and oh dear God -

Something came sharking towards him through the mists.

He jolted awake.

That could be her married name.

Panicked, he tried to prop himself up, and as he frantically felt for his mobile, that something which lurked in the depths of his mind turned over again and opened it eyes. He tried to think what it was.

For a day he waited, a year, a decade, a whole geological era.

Nothing came.

He strove to reason himself into tranquillity. *It isn't her, just someone like her. Stress is making you anxious.*

Yet somehow this reckoning did little to still the worms of apprehension that wriggled in his stomach.

Might it be her? What were the chances?

The *odds*?

His mind went back to an article he'd read not a long time ago while waiting at the barber's. Something to do with destiny, chance and coincidence.

The odds against the unlikely happening: ex-lovers sharing a lottery win, spouses colliding with each other on the highway, twins separated at birth choosing the same work, driving the same cars, naming their children Calvin, Hector and Gwynth and, oh dear God, fear and pain were building up, fighting for sovereignty of his body.

Fear won.

To quell it, he focused on the article. The odds, it declared, against these things happening are so high that when they do occur one can't help but think that unknown forces are at work.

Was it some unknown force - blind chance, fate, the furies - brought him to a hospital on the outskirts of Melbourne, to be slain by a woman who bore him a grudge?

No. The voice inside him was firm.

Because Eleanor Carson had never seen him.

How could she, behind his balaclava?

He held on tight to this belief, but deep in his brain a troublesome doubt assembled like a cloud. He flailed about till he found his phone, and as he began to message his wife, something smote him motionless.

A voice.

He listened, braced into frightened attention.

It came from outside his door.

Not just Irish, but Northern Irish.

Hers.

Gillespie held his breath and heard her spellbound.

The years rolled back.

He saw her house in South Belfast, the rain scoured glass of her patio door, the passage leading down to her kitchen with its smell of herbs and cooking meat, the Judge flinging back from the table, colour draining from his cheeks, his wife slewing round, her eyes on the muzzle of the Glock slowing lifting to look into his.

"Don't," she had pleaded. "Don't do it."

Gillespie whimpered, and the thought that no sane doctor would dare harm a patient, did little to diminish the immediacy of his terror.

What if a doctor were eaten with grief, and had carried with her the seeds of hate? What if she'd nothing to lose, no one to answer to, and was near the end of her career?

Fear, anxiety, guilt, remorse, all churned about inside him, but through it one salient thought pushed the others aside and got to the top of the welter: she had nothing to go on - only his build.

Yet something in Gillespie wouldn't be quieted.

He returned to her kitchen.

And as he tried to imagine what those blue eyes saw in the nano-second before he pulled the trigger - the thought that had crouched at the rim of his consciousness broke to the surface like a ten-day-old corpse.

A lightning bolt went through him.

But, no, he reasoned, impossible to see it from where she stood - in the midst of turmoil, *the face of death.*

And yet -

It was the one small defect that every

acquaintance, every colleague, every lover he'd ever had, had pounced on in a jocular way.

But you'd have to be near him to see it.

Eleanor Carson stood nine feet away.

Can you see someone's eyes from nine feet away?

The lashes that fringe them?

If so he was doomed.

For a crop of snowy lashes in a rank of ebony black had to be a syndrome.

Had she somehow clocked it – that quarter inch of silvery hairs? Noted the colour and shape of his eyes? And if she had, why not try to track him down?

He'd been a suspect. She could have nailed him.

To hang by your lashes.

Gillespie wasn't blind to the comedy of the situation, and under any other circumstances would have laughed. Now all he felt was a sinking of his heart that was the sickening premonition of disaster.

She had seen him earlier in A & E, looked into his eyes, and knew who he was. Through his pores, his antennae, and the hairs that stood out on the back of his neck, he felt this.

"Can I leave it with you, Mr Yoong?"

Outside his door her voice was rising and falling.

It was interrupted by another voice, but Gillespie no longer listened. A mist had come into the room, and a strange feeling overwhelmed him as of being in a dream.

He was alone, adrift in a hostile world.

Belfast seemed unreal and far away, a *War & Peace* novel with missing pages and crumbling covers. But it was home, and no matter how hard he worked, how far he strayed, he came back to it. He always would be coming back.

With a wrenching heart he stared across the room, his eyes blank, his thoughts so balanced between fear and bitterness as to fix him in an attitude of utter immobility.

He railed against Fate, the cards she dealt him, the games she played, the things she stooped to.

Did it amuse her to set him up with all he had hoped for - a name that nobody questioned, a country to come to anchor in, a woman, a job, a law degree from night school - then raise her hand to strike him down?

"And you have the x-rays, you say?"

Her voice was clearer now, for the door was pushing in.

He had an impression of tumbling backwards into

an abyss, but a sudden release of adrenaline constricted his consciousness to a laser-like focus.

He would appeal to the carer in her, address her in the language of the law.

"I know you know me, Dr Carson. I am sorry for who I am, for what I did. Being young and the victim of circumstances is no excuse. That said, I grew up in a place subjugated by fear. Terrorism brutalised the people in my community. Protection rackets decided who worked, who didn't. I was forced to fall in with the wrong set, do it their way - threaten, maim, deal with those who persistently put their members away."

He froze as she entered the room.

With a lab coat over her scrubs she looked imposing.

He was right in that this was Eleanor Carson, but - his heart gave one great bounding leap - wrong to imagine she knew him, for she was smiling as she padded towards him.

Her expression was one of concern tempered with goodwill, as of one who understands suffering and has the will and means to alleviate it.

"I'm sorry to keep you so long, but we're

hopelessly understaffed."

Her words, and the manner of their delivery, percolated his being with a delicious warmth.

Joy ran through his veins.

He felt nothing like this exaltation before in his life, this confidence in the inherent goodness of things except on the day he entered Australia on a passport that said he was Andrew McGill.

"How are you feeling?"

Gillespie grimaced in a way that tried to make it seem as if he wouldn't mind being out of there.

Dr Carson understood.

"We're taking you down to theatre now," she said, and when, after an infinitesimal pause she added, "Mr Gillespie", he experienced a curious sensation.

A bomb exploded somewhere near, as one had

done in North Belfast.

He underwent, as on that occasion, the same mind numbing reverberation, a paralysis, a violent shaking of his brain.

A hum arose in his ears so shrill as to nauseate him. And as the gurney was wheeled through the door, he realised that what was happening now was an epilogue to a story that started sixteen years earlier.

He looked away to the window, aware that a bird outside was keening, that the sky beyond was purple-pink, that the sun had slipped behind the hills, and would never shine for him again.

Journal of a Lower Master

Entry: *2nd day of October, 1891*

Dear, dear, trouble again with ladies.

But I was firm with this one - for she was not alone dogged, but persisted in presenting at the worst imaginable moment: the college under siege with an influx of foreign students - two of them *women*. An unforeseen change of staff, Swartz having succumbed to a bout of diphtheria; Bettinelli carried off to an asylum for the insane - crying out about the pig half-man, noise, battle, and fighting in the sky.

Poor old Betti. Nostradamus on the brain.

But back to the lady.

I had noticed her crossing the forecourt, and knew from the thrust of her jaw she had received my missive and felt aggrieved. Who really was she, I wondered, that she should dare approach the Academy - unchaperoned, and without an invitation? I turned from the window, excusing myself to the class, and hurried down the passage to my office.

I waited till she knocked and entered the room before taking my stand at the side of my desk. Then, chin cocked, hands behind my back, I militantly began an address distinguished for its lack of ambiguity.

"Pray, madam, have a seat. You will appreciate tutorials are under way, and being understaffed, I am sorely pressed for time. I will hasten therefore to the point. I am sorry to have to reiterate - we cannot hold on to your son. Not alone is he mentally sluggish, his behaviour is anti-social.

"I have had a note from your husband expressing surprise and wishing to know in what respect your son is disruptive. Your son - and this I cannot over-emphasize - is not disruptive as such. The very opposite is the case: he is silent to the point of being taciturn.

"Questions put to him are left unanswered. He has a way of staring that chills the blood. The arts, sciences, sports, technology - anything you wish to name - are matters to him of supreme unimportance.

"Our motto, as you know, is to turn information into knowledge and knowledge into practice. The only time your son has ever smiled was at mention of this motto. I speak, as you might imagine, more in sorrow than in anger. We hold no grudge against your son. But as we in this academy have standards to maintain, and do not envisage improvement, we have no choice but to send him down.

"You might, if you wish, apply to the Polytechnic.

"But I would not count on his being admitted.

"You ask have we any other suggestions? As it happens, we do. Considering his apathy and inability to interact or make decisions, something not overly taxing, where he is not called upon to speak. Farm labouring, say. Hotel or factory work.

"I am sorry, Frau Einstein, if this upsets you. The problem is, that for higher education one needs something to work on. And when it comes to having to think, *that* is where Albert falls down".

The lady rose and left the room, outrage written in every line of her. Manifestly, her son's brains are the only ones worth having.

Tiresome creatures, ladies.

How Do I Love Thee?

It was with hate in her heart that she boarded the train.

She plumped down onto the first available seat, not caring that her hair was askew, her eyelids swollen, and a sliver of something lacy looped out from the unzipped part of her Louis Vuitton holdall.

Nor did she care that her stomach growled and she hadn't showered in twenty-four hours.

She didn't care about anything.

For, two days earlier, the bottom fell out of her world.

She'd been shamed. Degraded.

Dragged in the most humiliating of dusts: that reserved for older women who allow themselves to be approached on amorous terms - by boys.

With a face hard as iron, she yanked back the zip of the holdall, trawled up a glossy and affected to read.

But she couldn't attend to the written word.

Her thoughts, even as her eyes read steadily down the page, went round and round in circles.

Why had she not seen it coming?

Where was logic? *Common sense?*

Surely she knew that the young man never existed who could love a woman twice his age?

And yet, for nineteen glorious months, despite that geography separated them, Garvin had shown unmistakable signs of wanting to woo her: gunning to Belfast on a borrowed Harley Davidson, inviting her to Dublin when his mates were out of town, hitching to Wicklow to be with her at the cottage.

Slim, with all the beauty of twenty-two years, he had come at a time when she needed him most, for Richard's affections had long since cooled. Not having children, and being an only child herself, her future had seemed like a long vista of empty years. Until the timely arrival of Youth -

"Ah, there you are," crashed into her thoughts.

Fran looked up with a swift expectancy.

A man was standing there. Sixty or thereabouts. Frieze of hair above his ears. Henry Kissinger spectacles.

"Don't mind, do you, I followed you onto the train?"

A good thing, thought Fran, as her eyes swept up his trifling details, it was day and not night, Connolly and not Penn Station, for a suspicious mind would find menace in such a question thrown out by a stranger. Yet the man seemed harmless enough and his question, she saw, did not demand an answer for he had already settled across from her, and was riffling through the pages of a dog-eared notebook.

Presently, he looked up.

Their eyes met.

"Saw you earlier, and...I was going to offer to carry that." He inclined his head towards her holdall. "You seemed a little shaken."

Was it her imagination or had the carriage fallen silent?

She let a moment pass, then "Thank you," she said, "but I'm perfectly fine." She held his gaze to the count of three, then back to her magazine.

And Garvin.

Her real grief was not so much finding him in the cottage making love to a girl still in her teens, but the way he had smiled on being caught in flagrante. Having that morning had her forehead plumped at a clinic in Dublin she had come to the cottage to rest before meeting with the youth the following day.

True, she had given him the key to the cottage, but strictly to work in.

For Garvin was a playwright, the merest tyro, who saw himself as the young man who, though undistinguished now in the eyes of the world, would reveal himself in due course as a latter-day Harold Pinter.

All he needed was a break. Which came in the shape of herself: she had fallen into his lap and he hadn't even shaken the tree.

And here he now was on her bed, smiling up through the kelp of his hair, his smile saying *I can have anyone for I am young and you shall forgive me.*

"Out," she'd said, in a voice not to be disputed, and inwardly bewailing that every one of the forty-six years Garvin knew were behind her showed on her pale and twitching face.

Fran came back to the moment for the train was pulling away, and as it bored its way through dark-walled cuttings that gave egress from the city, she saw in the glimmer of the window that her fellow passenger had lowered his chin and over his glasses was studying her.

She turned and met his examining gaze.

And because he was elderly and had seemed

concerned, and she felt she'd been needlessly rude, she made a comment on the weather which he returned with small talk of his own. He spoke with command in a plummy voice, one she recognised, Dubliner that she was, as the Belfast brahmin accent.

Then, "Lost my wife a year ago," he said, seemingly apropos of nothing and without a change of tone. On he chattered in a desultory manner, touching on other topics. Words that reached her were underwater-like for by now she was back with her own thoughts, elbow on the table, fist supporting her chin while she looked back on the last nineteen months with 20/20 hindsight.

Garvin might have admired, but he never loved her.

What he got from their relationship was her social usefulness. With a film director husband whose anti-war movie - *Presumed Alive* - was among those selected for the Palme d'Or Festival - she was a useful person for a playwright to know.

And she hadn't seen it coming because of being dazzled: the youth's first words on approaching her in the lobby of Hotel Martinez had lifted her up to a higher plane of ecstasy.

"You are without doubt the inspiration for your

husband's beautiful Herta."

Flattered, thrilled, she rewarded his compliment by introductions which would have seemed to a writer awesome - producers, directors, production company honchos.

The future playwright lost no time: might he interest Mr Goode in a screenplay?

"Sure. Of course -" Richard barely registered his presence. "Send on your script."

Whereupon Garvin, as though by some kind of legerdemain, whipped a manuscript from his pocket and handed it over.

Richard never read the script, and when, some weeks later, Garvin took to phoning the house, Fran was there to field his calls. Next came emails, then messages on her iPhone at intervals that were growing shorter.

All a matter of time before the young man declared he was coming north to see her.

Fool, fool, to be taken in.

Vanity of course had been the spur. A wish in her waning years still to feel power, still to have the assurance of her beauty.

Lost in these thoughts, the train by now had picked

up speed.

In moody abstraction, she watched the flitting landscape and thought of Richard who had left her for the proverbial younger model, using as an excuse that she was callous, cold, and narcissistic.

Conveniently forgotten was the part she had played in shaping his career before coming to roost in Belfast - networking, overseeing the business and financial decisions of his made-for-television features, his stage productions, and the motion picture that made his name.

"... and are, my dear, much my idea..."

Fran heaved a martyred sigh.

The man across from her was banging on, and although she would glance at him from time to time, nod here, wince there, she'd been aware only of the timbre of his voice and nothing else.

Tiresome. Boring.

But too late now to change her seat.

"...excuse myself on the grounds I am PROFESSOR of Classics at Queen's. Or *was*."

"Sorry - " Fran closed her magazine. "But I seem to have lost you on one of the roundabouts."

"I said you are much my idea of Helen of Troy."

Whether calculated to that end or not, the professor could not have said anything more likely to disarm Fran's hostility. She didn't dare let herself smile for fear of revealing how chuffed his words had made her.

She warmed to them, hardly caring if he meant them or not.

And as she shook her head in feigned exasperation, there drifted into her consciousness something from Austen her ex was fond of quoting and had used against her once or twice. *A lady's imagination is very rapid; it jumps from admiration to love, from love to matrimony in a moment.*

And indeed, as the other carried on with a disquisition on this the most inspiring woman in all literature, ancient and modern, a strange feeling came over her. A dreamy intoxication.

The professor seemed far away.

And she wasn't seeing him. Not really.

What she saw was something that ought to shame her, only it didn't.

It was a shimmering image of a possible future: an old world house set back from the road, high-ceilinged rooms and parquet floors, gatherings of the moneyed intelligentsia, charming compliments, elegant gestures, trips to Greece, to Alexandria -

And I shall love thee to the level of every day's most quiet need.

Her eyes focused.

She gazed at the professor.

They could be - assuming he was setting his cap in her direction - the most harmonious of companions. She would write off Richard as an error of judgment. He need never hear of Garvin.

Her eyes glistened.

To think of being wanted again. *Admired.*

Having someone pleased to be with her.

What a contrast to her recent experience. After the dark torments of the last few days she found at last she was smiling.

But as she was marshalling her forces getting ready to expatiate on the brighter side of her existence, the professor said something that staggered her.

"This train - is it going north or south?"

The question put continents between them.

"You mean you don't know?" she said, snappy in her anxiety.

The professor looked down at his notebook with

studied attention. Then, lifting his eyes, he gazed into hers.

No. He didn't know for sure. He had come to Dublin to visit his daughter only to remember at the eleventh hour she was married and living in Melbourne. Nothing for it but to turn around. Trouble was, he seemed to have dozed and then misplaced his luggage. To top it all, he had forgotten how to make his way home.

And with that, he showed her his notebook. On the fly leaf was the name of the place where he lived: a retirement home in Larne.

"You happen to know where it is?"

And now, of course, she understood; saw it all with a horrible clarity. She was once again a means to an end. Just as Garvin had used her to kick-start his career, this older man had latched on to her - manifestly a safe *matronly* woman - in the hopes she would lead him back to his fold. A shepherdess guiding a missing sheep.

Her thoughts shifted to Richard.

He had left her, had he not, because she was callous, cold, and narcissistic?

Well now, here was her chance to prove him wrong.

She turned to this elderly man with the short circuit in his brain and resolved to help him.

Yes. She would escort him off the train with words of reassurance, pilot him along the platform, up the escalator to the main body of the station. She would stop to report his missing luggage then take him by taxi to the care home in Larne.

The staff would commend her, as would her friends at the bridge club, her neighbours, the crew at the gym - even Richard should he get to hear of it.

A few years hence, a woman would present at her door, ask for Frances Helena Goode, remarking with a smile on the appropriateness of her last name.

"*In his will my father left you ...*"

The sun was low in the sky when the train pulled into Central Station.

Taking the old man by the arm - for he was nearer to seventy than sixty - she ushered him towards the exit, enjoining him to mind the step.

Lightly, she disengaged her hand then, shouldering her holdall, oozed ahead of him along the platform, weaving her way in and out among the commuters.

She took the escalator and without a backward

glance carried on briskly to the main body of the station.

From there to the taxi rank.

Ten minutes later, she drew an easier breath as she turned the key in her townhouse door.

Hamper

Xmas hamper
Signed anon
Wonder who
it could be from
Wine bottle full of grit
Ghastly word to rhyme with it

Chocolate box
Full of stones
A nasty tape
with moans and groans
Earl Grey tea box
Full of mud
Yule log
Just a dud

Two dead mice
In plum pud
Xmas crackers
No good
Note within from crazy jester
Food to suit my tax inspector

Checking Out

Because of my age I allow myself to be didactic, and few contradict me.

However, when it comes to the subject of death - planned death - what I refer to from time to time as SAE (Self Administered Euthanasia) - my friends, distressingly, have minds of their own. This I would not have found out had I not held my soirée.

It was the twenty-first day of June, my seventy-ninth birthday, and we were gathered in my small front parlour: Sally and Kate on the couch, Indira and myself on either side of the fireplace. On the coffee table was simple fare - nuts, 7 Up, sherry, and the rock buns Darren made the night before. I was the oldest person in the room, and holding forth on cremation.

"I rather suspect that what goes up in smoke`, I said," are the corpses and not the coffins. I mean, why would they incinerate five or six hundred pounds worth of pinewood, with inlay, brass handles, a breast plate -"

"Yes, and lining," piped Sally, as she gulped her Bristol Cream.

"And lining," I inclined my head in Sally's

direction. "If you ask me they turn the bodies out, wipe the coffins down, and when the dust - quite literally - settles, sell them back to the undertakers."

"Whose idea it was in the first place?" said Sally, whistling a little through her dentures.

"I half admire their enterprise," I carried on. "But they'll not be getting much from me. I've already ordered my cardboard box - reinforced in case you're worrying. No lining, no frills. Oh, and a woolly shawl for over the box." I stopped to ponder this for a moment. "Comforting, isn't it, the thought of wool?"

"Well now, Lizzie," said Kate, putting down her glass, and wiping her mouth with her mottled hand. "I hope the moths get the box and the shawl long before you need them."

"Thank you," I said, in my best Bette Davis, and smoothing the folds of my dress. "But as a matter of fact I'll be checking out in exactly a year."

Silence fell on the room, broken only by the slow tick of the mantle clock which seemed to me to say: *What Rot.*

I said, "Don't look so morose, people are dying all the time."

Indira leaned forward in the wing chair, and brushed a crumb from her sari. "How can you possibly predict when you're going to die?"

"I'm not predicting," I said. "I'm saying."

Sally sat up electrified. "What does that mean exactly?"

Anyone who didn't know Sally Higgins well would have missed the trace of excitement in her voice. Hers was a life of predictable days and predictable nights since cancer swept her Harold away, so that anything that broke their monotony was greatly welcomed.

"You're not sick or anything, are you?"

"No. Which is why I'm making plans."

"I don't understand," said Indira, on whom facts of a disturbing nature were beginning to press.

"I am exiting," I said. "*Going*, in other words. This day next year to be precise. On my eightieth."

"And how d'you propose doing that?" asked Kate. who like Sally. was sixty-eight and had a taste for the macabre.

I looked from one of them to the other, surprised they couldn't see it my way, and vexed with myself for bringing the subject up. Time enough until May of next year. Serious trouble if Social Services got even a whiff of what I had I mind.

"Well, Lizzie?"

I glanced up. Six round eyes were looking to me for a response.

I heaved a martyred sigh. "A snort of cocaine," I said flatly, "and that will be it."

Indira horse laughed. "You hear that everyone? Coffin, cocaine, and cremation."

Wincing, I sipped my sherry, glanced at the clock, and realised that the quietness this time had to do with a paroxysm: the trio were doubled over in a fit of silent laughter. They wheezed, they twitched, they looked at me through shrivelled lids. And my face, watching them without a smile, touched off a volley of shrill nervous laughter.

I excused them on the grounds that the way Indira put it, it was rather funny, and repeated the words to myself: *Coffin, Cocaine and Cremation*. And yes, I decided, rhythm.

It positively pulsed with rhythm - that, appropriately enough, of the funeral march. You could almost hear the roll of the drum. On the other hand - I cast a glance at the Bristol Cream -

"I am Perfectly Serious," instantly restored them to order.

Sally pushed her teeth back into place. "You can't take your own life, Lizzie. It wudden be right. A terrible thing to be even thinking."

I sank back onto the cushions, and metered my words out slowly: "A snort of cocaine and that will be it."

A frost descended on the trio. They looked at me, looked at each other, looked at me again.

"And what would *you* know about cocaine?"

I turned to Indira. Seventy, majestic, a total abstainer, and a bit of a fly in the birthday ointment. I wondered why I asked her.

"Not much," I said, in the clipped tone of the former teacher, and passed her the plate of buns. "But enough to know it's not the worst way you could go - buzz, a sublime feeling of well-being, you're gone. And never get to find it out."

Sally suddenly flashed her gums. "You might like it so much you'll not want to go. My grandson -"

"No, no," Indira left off chewing and took a sip of 7 Up. "You take cocaine, and I promise you you'll lose the plot - delusions, fits, paranoia -"

I clucked with impatience. "Did I mention surviving the snort?"

"But you're only fooling, of course," said Kate in a quavering voice, draining her glass to its dregs.

"Absolutely not." I pushed myself out of my chair, topped up their drinks, set the bottle down with a small symbolic bang. "It's what I said - a party, cocaine will be the focus, Darren will see to the coffin, the following day they cremate me." I threw my head back with the air of one not to be defied. "I am exiting at precisely midnight twelve months from now - "

"If God spares you," said Indira, giggling in a manner unlike her. I gazed at her uneasily for a moment, and was about to comment when the pair on the couch broke out together.

"And what about the undiscovered country?" said Kate, who had literary leanings, having worked all her life in a library.

"Strange whim to seize you, dear," Sally's voice climbed over Kate's. "My grandson -"

"She doesn't mean it." Indira sat up in a swish of silk. "Attending your own funeral. I *ask* you."

But she was wrong.

I meant it.

The thought of bowing out was a comfort - especially the way I had planned it. For with that thought - and I know that someone said this before me - a calm passage is to be made across many a bad night. No. I would go on the night of my eightieth. And with a bang.

"But you must be depressed," said Sally, "to be even thinking this way."

"Prudent," I said, "not depressed."

"All them books you haven't read, the places you haven't seen, and what if God is up there looking cross?"

I thought of God, the one I'd learnt about at school. Rancorous, always needing to be placated, full of spite and anger unutterable. Bringing down brimstone, burning bushes, causing floods, making accusations - in Darren-speak, a bit of an arse. Opposite of the one He would have us despise - poor old much maligned Satan. Who, for all his faults, was

never known to lose his cool. Liked his comforts by all accounts, snug place with open fires; no breezes, damp clouds or pious martyrs doing meek.

"Terrible way to celebrate your seventy-ninth,"

recalled me.

"Yes, Kate. I know. But I'm not prepared to go the way of Maisie."

We were silent a moment, contemplating the mother of five, mortared into a wheelchair, food drooling from the side of her mouth, hand contracted into a cone.

I raised my elbow to empty my glass of sherry. "Just think of it," I said, "The last lap of your life to be spent in a home, in a Pamper's pad, helpless, patronised by annoyingly cheery staff who feed you, wash you, and at the same time every day prop you up on a cold, steel -"

"Motherfucker bedpan."

Everyone froze. All eyes turned on Indira.

"Well now," said Sally who had as a son a priest, and whose brother-in-law was bishop of Albany. "Where you come from it might be quite all right to - "

"Sorry." Indira's grin was sheepish. "But I always wanted to say that word."

We didn't laugh.

We brayed.

A sustained eruption of guffaws where Sally's teeth slipped out again. It took a long time to settle back, and I was passing round the Kleenex when the guffaws started up again. We squealed, our shoulders shook, tears came streaming down our cheeks. And a bottle of sherry and six rock buns later we were getting totally out of hand.

"Scrotum," bawled Sally, with the wicked joy of the wrongdoer.

"Bollocks," squealed Kate before toppling over on Sally's lap.

Indira seemed to be weeping. "Would you stop, you will give me a prolapse."

It was the longest day of the year but twilight was creeping into the room. I lit the spiced berry candle on the mantelpiece and, after checking everyone's drink, told them my plans for the following year.

The plot in my small back yard which did duty as a lawn would be dug up at once and a swimming pool put in its place. The tool shed would serve as the poolside bar, the patio would be hung about with loungers, tables with matching umbrellas and tubs of scarlet geranium.

"But, Lizzie dear - "

"The dining room will hold the buffet food. And this," I spread my hands to indicate the parlour, "will make a smaller inside bar. Lift the rug and there's your dance floor."

"Yes, but Lizzie - "

"Balloons at the front of the house, pots of hydrangeas all the way down to the garden gate, fairy lights on the box hedge."

"Right, but Lizzie - "

"I'll be shelling out for a Jaeger dress, black as befits the occasion. Hairdo, pearls. Lick of varnish on the nails."

"Yes but - "

"The party, of course, will start at three, by then I'll be into my second joint. Yes, you heard me. *Joint.* Darren has given me his word. And no, Indira, he's not a dissolute but we'll get to that later on."

"Lizzie - "

"I mentioned, didn't I, the string quartet? Not sure where to put them, but I'm going to have them play Mozart. Not his Requiem, no. That would be morose. Something lively like his polkas."

"*Lizzie?*"

I turned to this current of constant interruption. Sally was leaning towards me, jaw sagging, mouth pursed into a cat's behind.

"Did you say ... a *swimming* pool? In yer back yard?"

I closed my eyes in a gesture of patient suffering, opened them to say: "Why not, if I have the money? I have a pension, you know, savings - "

"But all this outlay for a few hours a horsin' around? When you think a people in Bangladesh, and missionaries who wudden mind a couple a extra bob for digging wells in - "

"Ledder finish, would you?" Kate by now had lost command of her tongue. She looked from me to Sally and back. "String quartet," she prompted.

"Yes, and the coffin meanwhile will be spirited away in the garage. We eat, we drink, make merry. At midnight the cake will make its appearance. Not one of your great big white - "

"Motherfucker - "

I graciously bowed towards Indira. "Motherfucker eighty-candles all ablaze kind of things ..." They laughed like drains not at the word but my deadpan face as I said it. "...but a Mars Bar-sized cake of the finest blow."

"*Cocaine*," said Indira, rolling her eyes when Sally started up again.

"It mightn't be wise, but, if you like you may join me. Straws, knives, and doll-house spoons set out on a silver platter." I looked down at my glass with studied attention. "We snort, we dance, and weather permitting, skinny dip in my heated pool." I sighed, lifted my brows, and stared across the room. "I often dreamt of doing that. And indeed if I'd any brains I'd have had a dress rehearsal this year."

"You're actually serious?" said Indira, on a high, incredulous note and coughing into her fist. "You really mean this?"

"Why wouldn't she?" Kate belched softly, and leaning over, clawed up a fistful of nuts. "A free spirit, isn't she? No family apart from the nephews, laughs whenever you mention God - "

"You know what it is," said Sally, eyeing me beadily over her glasses. "I've only to think a Maisie to want to join you." Her jaw chopped. "Go on about the party. I take it there won't be any young folks?"

"No," I said. "Over sixties strictly. Until I need to send for Darren. Which reminds me, I'll have to learn to use an iPhone."

"Yes," said Sally. "And take it with you in the coffin. Just in case."

Indira whinnied. "They'll be glad to see it at the crematorium."

"And so..." Kate examined a point in space a foot or two from her nose. "…what are you planning to do with the house?"

"I'm leaving it to Darren."

She stopped mid chew. "Your nephew's son? Bald young man who calls you doll?"

"Tattoo on the back of his head?" chimed Sally, her voice a careful balance between shock and condemnation.

"Did I hear he was up for growing pot?" said Indira, sticking the knife in the wound and giving it a wiggle.

"Hmm, well …" I lifted the plate and held it out. One rock bun remained. The trio ignored it. "He is a little feckless, I'll admit. But honest. *And* funny. There whenever I need him. And knows to mind his business."

It was in their eyes I was being a fool to imagine that anyone could possibly love the elderly just for themselves. I touched a hand to my hair, and thought of all the old folks I'd known as a girl: pensioners in the street, nuns in their convents, friends of my parents and grandparents. I thought of Grandma Mooney who came to live with us towards the end. Had I liked her? Loved her? Given her any thought at all?

Not really, if I'm honest.

In my forties I realised, too late, that Miriam Mooney had been not just interesting but a quite exceptional beauty - a teacher of music, ballerina posture, amber eyes and flaxen hair. Sought after, postman daily at her door, young men swooning and dropping at her feet.

A shame to never have had a proper conversation, to not have known then what I know now.

"Grandma," I would say, "You were a beauty, were you not? And so much in demand. And see what happened - the years slipping by, each one a little less warm than the year before, each one slowly, imperceptibly, stripping you of your assets, your admirers gradually dropping off like your teeth and your hair, so that here you are at eighty, sipping cocoa, stroking the cat, staring dreamily into the fire."

Is it possible, I would wonder, to be content with so little, to be relieved of all the things which made life worthwhile, and not want to die?`

My thoughts switched sadly to another elderly person.

Not so good looking, Granny McMaster. Nobody falling at her feet, not even Vinney who, by asking her to marry him, had assumed he was offering her an anchor, poor old Maud being very plain. Her fat little head sitting on her body without the benefit of a neck.

And her mouth - permanently fixed into a cross little bag.

Sad, I thought, to be vexed for whatever reason when serenity is what age should bring. Repose, like that enjoyed by Grandma Mooney.

Peace.

And even, dare I say it, flavour?

Like a peach in the sun, old folks ought to hang on the afternoon wall of life. And then we'd remember them kindly. The way I'd like to be remembered myself. The way I suspect I will be.

By Darren, if no one else.

Darren.

Guileless, trusting. Never looking for hidden motives.

Not academic, it was true, but charitable, good with his hands, donor card in his wallet, regularly giving his fresh young blood, sponsoring a child in Bolivia, pins in his ear, rings in his nose, yet writhing with the effort not to weep as the lid was lowered on his grandma's coffin.

Dear young person.

Calling on me every day, moving about my house with the endearing air of one who belongs, whistling, taking out my bins, fetching my pension, cooking me Bolognese, playing chess, waltzing me round the parlour, taking the cat to the vet, channel hopping, tinkering with that motorbike of his, debating,
contradicting, landing me pretend clips on the jaw, buying me a helmet for my seventieth and - up to recently, and quite without embarrassment - whisking me off for rides on the bike.

Yes, he would get the house. And everything in it.

"But Lizzie dear," said Sally, turning the conversation, "You'll not enjoy your birthday if you know you're going to die."

You'll not enjoy your birthday if you know you're going to die.`

Well, now, speaking as a former teacher, figure-of-speechwise, what, I asked myself, would that be a line of? To think I cannot remember. Darren would know. An A in English for all his messing. An A Star, as a matter of fact. And for that his amazed father gave me all the credit.

The silly man.

With his pinstripe suits, patterned ties, briefcase, and assumption that as a barrister his are the only brains worth having. Oh, how I'd like to look him in the eye: *What your son has, Henry Matthews, you could never hope to buy.*

"Did you hear me?"

I blinked. "What? Not enjoy my birthday? Of course I will," I said, on a note high enough to shatter their glasses. "Every moment of it. I will exit on the biggest high known to God or man."

Sally was mutinous. "Deep down, Lizzie dear, you must be sad to ever a got that thought in the first place."

For once the others didn't interpose.

That I was sad was in their eyes, too. Sad, an arid old maid, never having had a family, never having had a man. My nephew's son the only one to show an interest.

God only knows what scenes of dark misery and past gloom my plans and appearance must suggest to them. In their imaginings Miss Mooney has always been as she is now: shrivelled, unloved, alone, her nearest of kin and their partners patiently waiting for her to die.

I suppose they would hold a jealous reproach against me for enjoying myself in a world that holds so little joy for them. Naturally optimistic, uncritical, easy to please, I respond to all the gentle pleasures that life has on offer from iced lollies to rides on motorbikes, to daffodils in my garden, to works of art, to music, television, books and food and drink.

Not so for the three old fogies whose idea of what is fitting in an eighty-year-old is that she should regularly visit her church, doze in her chair in the afternoons, sit about chewing her gums, while she waits for her Blessed Lord to call her home to whatever damp cloud she'll have to sit on for eternity.

Pitying *me.*

I, who for twenty glorious months had a lover.

Still have him.

Gone, it is true, behind the clanking gates of death.

Wrenched from my arms on the eve of our wedding. But with me, near me, hardwired into my soul.

You would laugh, ladies, would you not, at the thought of a dried-up Lizzie ever having loved a man? Stamp your feet on the floor were I to tell you I was mistaken once for Ingrid Bergman. Oh yes, onboard a ship on a cold October afternoon. I can see it as clearly as though it happened the week before last.

The tall young girl gripping the rails of the deck, staring forlornly into the sea; turning when a low voice asked if she weren't the Swedish actress.

His eyes, the colour of the sky in June.

For how long I gazed at them I will never know. Then, "No," I said. "I'm not Ingrid Bergman. But thank you for the compliment." And as something more seem demanded of me: "I'm Elizabeth Mooney, a humble teacher, and I'm sure you'll not have to guess where I'm from."

He seemed to study me for a moment, slightly at a

loss for words.

And while he did, I studied him.

Australian, his beautifully tailored suit deceptively ascetic; beneath it his figure slim with a taut economy of line bespeaking hard work, meals that were often missed and he knew perfectly well I wasn't Ingrid Bergman. What would she be doing in the slums of a ship?

"You are travelling alone?"

I nodded. But my face was flushed, for suddenly I was intensely aware of this obviously first class passenger: of his mouth, the spacing of his eyes, the aroma of tobacco which hung about him, his dark tie flapping over his shoulder, his hair slapping round his head in the cold Atlantic breeze.

Looking into the stranger's eyes, clasping the hand he was holding out, it was as if something had moved in its sleep inside me and heaved a little sigh.

Osbourne, the young man said, with an earnest gravity that made me smile. Richard Osbourne. Journalist with The Guardian. Covered the war from Rome - '43 to '45. Couldn't settle after that, Washington Post offered him work, going to see how it figured out.

He stopped, looked at me.

"What part of the States are you going to?"

I blushed. He smiled.

It was a perception numbing moment, that first sighting of Richard Osbourne's smile. And for a brief period in time I lost touch with my surroundings - the rails I stood at, the throb of the engines, the spume churning up from the sea, the chill October wind whipping my coat about me, the wheel of the gulls as the boat moved further out to sea.

Then the world came back into place and I was calm, telling the young man Albany, that my mother's sister would meet me, that a job awaited me at a high school in Troy, that my mother hoped I wouldn't like America, that -

I left off speaking, suddenly shy of him.

Three days later we were lovers. And I never got to work in Troy. Instead I took up a teaching post in Washington and went and lived with Richard. One year after that, I was back in Ireland without him.

But not really, I told myself over and over.

Forty-eight years since Richard died in his motor, but still he is with me, sharing my inner life, spending hours talking to me, teasing, raising his eyebrows at Darren, asking if I didn't consider that the blue-eyed biker looked just a little like himself - the shoulders, the set of his head, the spacing of his eyes, the slow smile spreading across his face, glancing like that, sideways out of his lashes?

And of course I would round on Richard with a fury. That bald young man - who smokes, grows pot, guns down the road on a motorbike - resembling *you*, a preppy prince, who never missed a day from school, who went to college, to war, to the States?

You old silly, I would add. He isn't remotely like you. Not even the colour of his eyes. Well...just a little, perhaps. His are periwinkle blue, and yours... well, they were a little paler. *Or was it darker*?

I swallowed, glanced across at my three old friends, surprised to find them slightly blurred. I blinked and - there - it was quite all right again.

But to pity me. Pity *me*.

Who, five years after Richard, had come across Ambrose. As great a contrast to my darling Richard as the Cretaceous period was to the Jurassic period that went before it.

But a good-looking man who taught religious education in my school.   Declaring he couldn't be anywhere I was not. That he would chuck the whole lot up - wife, child, job, and come and be my gardener if only he could see me once in a while.

You wouldn't care to hear that, ladies, would you? Shrivelled up Lizzie having two admirers?

Would it gratify you to know that on the day when I finally gave the nod, Ambi upped and returned to Molly, and had four more children after that?

But no, ladies, not alone.

Not arid. Not even sad.

In the absence of my one true love I took comfort in literature from Chaucer all the way up to Cheever, experiencing things you, I guess, will never know - oh, vicariously, I will admit - journeys through the past and into the future, illicit love, passionate wooings, ravishings set to the music of Handel and the rhythm of galloping horses, revolutions, enlightenment, adventures in Outer Mongolia - everything that literature has on offer and which is there if you would but take the time to see.

So don't be sorry for me, you tired old pillars of society. What I had with Richard you have never had with anyone, not with Harold - I glanced at Sally; not with Denis - I turned to Kate; and not with Sanjiv, your dote of a husband, Indira.

But cheer up. Now - at once.

I will carry on for another year, delighting in every moment, while delving a little into the past. And who knows, might I not - moments after my big send-off - open my eyes - my spiritual eyes - and see him? His slow smile, his floppy hair, his blue eyes looking into mine, placidly coming towards me.

All this I idly mused on as I listened dreamily to

my old friends quietly chatter.

The parlour, which for a while seemed to have quietened, recovered its breath and began to resound with new sounds. They were singing, wishing me well, and signalling an end to the evening.

"Happy birthday, Lizzie dearest."

"And many of them."

"You may put those plans of yours aside - "

"We'll review them for your ninetieth."

After they'd left I gathered up plates and moved along the passage to the kitchen. The back door opened and Darren stepped in.

"Well, doll..." He frowned at the chaos in the kitchen. "How'd it go?"

"Yes, well, I suppose I enjoyed it."

"So much so," his lip was lifting. "You might hang on another while? Get some value from your pool?"

I narrowed my eyes and stared at him sternly. "Decline the fifth proposition of the third book of Euclid and I'll tell you."

He laughed, picked up the last of the rock buns, sniffed and wiggled his eyebrows.

"They were fine if that's what you're asking." I slapped a dishcloth into his hands. "But see for next time? More currants, less spice. And for Jesus' sake go easy with the hash. I had a terrible time with Indira."

The Stars At Night

Good Evening, Patrick Moore here
I have news you won't believe
I've just nipped back from Pluto
Having taken special leave

It's a place we've overlooked
There's life there after all
The Plutonians are a marvel
If only 2 feet tall

They've got those dandy telescopes
A dozen miles in girth
And a hazy film surrounds their world
To hide from planet earth

They've made this special head gear
To help me breathe their air
And all of them are hairless
And only have one ear

Their fruit is most inspiring
It's made from chewy steel
You whip them down with laser jets
But only eat the peel

Their newborns are a study
They walk when six hours old
And their sweetie shops sell Earth Bars
And Earth Balls, so I'm told

I'm going to live much longer
If I stay among this race
And they've promised that they'll take me
On a ten-year trip through space

I'll report back when I can
Though this always causes strife
The only thing that bugs me
Since I found myself a wife.

Butter Pats and Climbing Roses

It was just the ticket, this grand little semi-D.

A stone's throw from Dollymount beach. Green front door. Flagged path leading up to a porch *studded* with climbing roses.

Never - not in a month of Sundays - would you find a more chocolate box setting within sight and sound of the sea. So we bought it. And then panicked. You see, it'd been on the market three times in seven years, and sold for what even we poor greenhorns considered a song.

Where, we wondered, was the catch?

True, the floorboards sagged, the kitchen reeked, the loo was out the back, but - these were things you could easily fix.

"Oh, why worry."

This from himself.

You should've seen him, staggering under the weight of a box of crockery. Shuffling crates across the floor. All pleased the delivery guys were gone, and we were alone at last with our bits and bobs.

"Whaddaya say, we stick on a record and put things away?"

It was the summer of '75, and we set to work to the soundtrack of *Love Me Do* on our decca record player - back then the height of musical technology. Forgetting our worries, we opened a crate and dug up our treasures, all the time planning the things we would do: update the kitchen, rip up the lino, fix the floorboards, install a bathroom.

Suddenly, I felt this surge of elation, for the years lay spread out before us. Large white canvasses on which we would paint the brilliant pictures of our lives. One such picture was me laying this table, decorating it with roses, setting butter pats out on a dish, pouring tea from the teapot that was still in the crate.

Poor fool me.

For I hadn't reckoned with Fate.

Yes, you heard me. *Fate*. That great old grudger of joys. Show any signs of being happy and I promise you, she'll go out of her way to get you. And oh, did she get me. For even as I was trawling up the teapot, there she was, the kill-joy, slowly rolling her sleeves up, getting ready to strike.

"WELKOM-to-the-neighbourhood-didn't-I-see-the-van-outside-and-I-figgered-ye'd-be-up-to-yeer-eyes-so-I'm-here-to-give-ye-a-hand."

Our hearts sank down beneath the floorboards, for here, we guessed, was the neighbour from hell. The one with her foot in your door. Grittily determined to help you - *whether you wanted her or not.*

Squaring our shoulders, we thanked her, and tried to dismiss her.

But she was firmly planted in the hall. Rapidly talking. Words gushing from her as from a geyser.

On-and-on-on she went.

And when we saw that no amount of patient waiting would bring her any nearer to the end of what she had to say, we were forced to take our coats off, as it were, plunge in the middle of the flow and convey to her somehow that we didn't need help.

Imagine us that first night, lying awake, knowing now what the catch was. We talked at intervals, discussing strategies. But plan how we might, there was no escaping our neighbour who called so often we glued a thimble over the doorbell, refused to answer her raps on the door, and stole about quietly so as not to alert her - prisoners in our own house.

Goes without saying, we never fully unloaded our crates, and a year would go by before we'd pack up again and move to a new place.

Tiny. Terraced.

Snatch of garden round the back.

No path. Porch. Or climbing roses.

What we *did* have was peace.

And neighbours who came to be friends. And who - when our kids would squabble in the street - would either smile and shake their heads, or give their best ever show of not having heard.

The Constitutional

It was a beautiful day, and Reginald's haemorrhoids hadn't troubled him in over a week, and the dog showed signs of settling down, and we'd found a fiver coming out of Tesco's, and I was humping most of the bags, and the breeze on the cliff road was bracing, yet here Reggie was -

Being angry.

Livid.

His face congested, his lips wire thin as he struck out for the upper reaches of Creggie Dubh, Jethro straining at the leash, Reggie calling over his shoulder that only low life women snuck alcohol into the groceries.

"Eleven a clock in the morning…closet drinker or what…next thing you'll tell me you're smoking, too."

My yellow headscarf flapped in the breeze, beating time to Reggie's words which sounded in my ears like dramatic chanting, the opening bars of Carmina Burana.

My eyes glazed.

I had a fleeting image of myself in the opening

credits of a big budget movie. Set to *O Fortuna* and the rhythm of galloping horses, I was Cathy spurring my gelding, hair streaming behind as I tried to catch up with the sinned-against Heathcliff.

I stopped, set down my bags, and rested my arms.

Then as Reggie carried on simultaneously scolding and untangling himself from the leash, I stuffed the kitchen rolls between the Chablis and the olive oil to stop the clinking that had touched off such a profoundly hostile reaction in Reggie.

I had blushed a vivid beetroot at the supermarket when the checkout girl looked first at me, then at Reggie who had materialised at my side and clucked with annoyance on seeing the wine. Had mother been with me, she'd have wheeled around on hearing that cluck, smiled with all her teeth, then, in a mock delighted voice: "Sadie, guess who's here to help with the bags?"

And I wondered, as I picked up my shopping and carried on again, how she'd react to Reggie's latest caper - the Rottweiler he took home without a word to me: a beast that was given to snarling, hadn't been trained, and was allowed the freedom of the house.

Mother would have no hesitation in sending it

packing.

Not for her to knuckle under, find herself smouldering, rehearsing the things she would say for when her husband was in a receptive mood: *doesn't it bother you, Reggie, that I have always been afraid of dogs? Don't you ever think of anyone but yourself? Don't you mind the neighbours complaining?*

Oh yes.

I was brave as mother during those silent rehearsals, and stood up to Reggie, and squared my shoulders, and withered him with a look.

Out loud and to his face I was a rabbit in a trance before an outsized cobra.

For Reggie was large and had a way of staring that froze the marrow.

He was prickly, easily upset.

And I would find myself, under his cold and hostile eye, talking in a wheedling voice, altering the script, stammering and tripping up - everything I was saying landing me in fresh difficulties.

So that it was impossible with Reggie to properly read the riot act.

Following my one and only protest - *I cannot*

have him in the house - Reggie's face had worked, his nostrils twitched, a vein began to bulge on his temple as he gave rein to his fury. I was to go and do some work, idle woman that I was, go back to my sewing, and stop focusing on things that didn't concern me.

Right.

Ignore the brute.

Was that the idea?

Pretend he wasn't there?

And if I was all that worried, I had a broom there, hadn't I, to ward him off ?

At the vision of myself looking over my shoulder first at my husband, then at his dog, resentment began to build and pound inside me like an abscess.

But it was Reggie I railed against, not his dog.

Reggie I really feared.

I ought never to have married a man I was afraid of. But once having done so, 1 should have made a stand, or at the very least laid down some rules. And

stuck to them. Or better still, have walked away.

My anger became less violent now, for I was rather breathless climbing the hill.

I stopped for a second time, pulled down my scarf

and let it wag about my neck.

The sun was high in a cloudless sky, the breeze energising, and, really, one ought to be glad for being alive and not do victim.

Yet victim I felt myself to be, for there was no comfort with Reggie, no hours of freedom, no moments of quiet, now he was honourably discharged from the Army. He seemed to be everywhere at once, dogging my every step, nothing escaping his vigilant eye.

Shocked he had been to discover, for instance, that mother would visit three times a week and that for nine months of the year for twenty-five years I'd had the central heating on to warm her in his absence. That thought enraged him, and brought a hornet's nest about my ears. *If we were occupied enough, we wouldn't feel the cold. Had we any idea of the price of oil?* And on he would go. And afraid to further inflame him, I wouldn't answer.

Think of it, afraid to inflame.

I, who singlehandedly managed a farm, put cattle out to graze, haggled at market, even learnt to drive a tractor.

Afraid to inflame.

Cowering whenever my husband would scold me.

Well -

I had no one to blame but myself. I should have nipped him at the very start.

"My dear, you don't mean to tell me you actually - *drink*?"

Thus said Reggie on our second date, when, following a five mile tramp through the country, I suggested we stop at the *Dog and Duck* to warm ourselves with a glass of port.

"Bad enough you don't attend to the Lord, but to actually enter a *public house*? And enter it - on the Sabbath?"

It was my warning, my chance to end it.

To walk away.

Only I didn't because of having nowhere to hurry to, only the farm.

No one to go to, only mother.

Up until Reggie, mine had been a humdrum life, a life of drudgery, my future a vast cold sea over which I would have to sail, wave after endless wave, lonely and adrift. And into that humdrum life had come Reggie, a lifeboat cutting across the sea - to offer me an anchor.

In the circumstances, could I be blamed for reaching out and saying yes?

All this flashed across my mind as, once again, I trailed after Reggie whose tall, erect figure was labouring up the hill.

Poor unhappy Reggie.

Finding out with a pang that the woman he had married was not alone not a model of blamelessness, but her mother was every bit as bad, indeed the root cause of the daughter's problem.

For mother was known to help herself nightly to what she referred to as a tot. Even suggested Reggie might like to help himself too.

"You'd be surprised," she told him after a particularly noisy flare-up - "the difference a wee tot would make to your opinions."

A vulgar harpie, he later called her.

A Jezebel.

To which I replied, in my cajoling voice, "I'm afraid, Reggie, you're not that keen on women, are you?"

I heaved a martyred sigh. And as I glanced at Reggie's departing back, I was visited by a distressing thought: Reggie was what he was - severe, critical, grudging of happiness, because there wasn't a soul in the world who loved him.

Not even his wife.

A devoted wife would have done wonders to tease out the goodness in a man, assuming he had some goodness in him. A really good wife could, if she wished, have performed miracles.

Clearly I wasn't a good enough wife.

But, if I really tried I could make improvements. Accept things as they were. Turn a blind eye to Reggie's tantrums, lower my expectations, not reach too far into the future.

"Is that not so?"

I turned towards the voice, aware that Reggie had crested the hill and was bawling out words most of which were lost in the wind. Words it might be better for me not to hear if his stance and the set of his shoulders were anything to go by.

Poor Reggie.

So quarrelsome.

A flavour of hostility in everything he said.

And no -

Not even a wholly devoted wife, not even ten

wives working on him in relays, could change the way Reggie was made. For, let us be honest, he was born a complainer, hair-triggered to be offended, primed to explode at the least provocation.

Any wonder he gravitated into the army.

Look at him, slewing round once again, shaking his fist, angrily reining in the dog. All that noise and clamour when he might be enjoying the day, the bracing air, the pound of the sea, the wheel of the gulls.

My thoughts shifted to mother who was fond of seagulls, and liked being up here in the summer, and would often insist on bringing a picnic.

Abruptly, at the thought of never seeing her again, my throat tightened. Strange too, that here, near the edge of the cliff, I had this sense of her being near, hovering around me. Gone to be sure behind the clanking gates of death, yet <u>there</u> was her voice in my ears.

"*Why did you marry him?*"

It been the last thing she had said before staging her farewell.

All the things she'd left unsaid were clearly written in every line of her: *you are a poor tethered creature, Sadie my girl. The crowning cowardice of your life your fear of standing up to him.*

"Why, Sadie, *why*?"

Although flaring with indignation, I'd given my best show of plumping her pillows.

"He was handsome, mother. And his job was good."

Mother stared at me chicken-faced, her blue eyes aiming into mine. I knew what those eyes saw: A Sergeant Major for a son-in-law, a big burly man unable to leave the parade ground. Bawling out orders on arriving home. Directing, enjoining, running my life like he might his troops, method and efficiency being what he craved. They were to blaze at him from every dusted shelf, every polished surface, every tap and doorknob.

Dawn raids into various rooms - scullery, sewing room, bathroom and attic - were not an uncommon occurrence, and I would wince as he'd round on me for what he'd call my disarray, my lack of pride in my appearance, my pigheaded indifference to all he was saying, my tardiness with meals, and worse than any of these, my reluctance to attend to the Lord on the Sabbath.

But it wasn't for any of these that mother had not liked Reggie.

No.

What mother hadn't liked were the bruises which were showing on various parts of me at intervals that were growing shorter, and for which I'd invariably put forward explanations

Hearing them, mother's lip would curl with derision.

Terrible for her to have fallen ill and have to live with us before she died. Away from Reggie she had only a vague idea of his possibilities. Nor had she dreamed how small a part reason played in his make-up.

I shrivelled to think of the things she'd found out that I had tried to hide, and the deceptions I was forced to resort to. That her son-in-law was a man of moods she already knew. That he was handy with his fist she was beginning to suspect.

"Why did you marry him when there was Mikey?"

Ah yes. Poor Mikey, in his little shop.

A grocery that expanded ten years on into a supermarket that, with the passage of time, became the property of Tesco. To think how easy my life would have been. Children, guaranteed to break ice, bring new friends into our lives, and be a comfort to us in our old age.

And in the meantime no counting of pennies, squirreling away of pensions, doing without fires in the so-called summer months, going for walks that I didn't like, looking over my shoulder, hiding my cache of Fruit & Nut, sneaking Chablis into the house, afraid to store it in the fridge, Reggie being certain to see it.

Dreadful, dreadful, having to go to the sewing room to pour myself a glass on Friday afternoons, my eye on the door and my ears pricked until it was safely swallowed and the glass washed and stowed away.

I, who was a McTaggart, Scotland in my ancestry in the shape of fiery, red-haired, claymore wielding Highlanders.

Look at me, this lovely April morning, smiling anxiously at my husband, trotting after him like a lapdog, trudging up the cliff road with heavy Tesco bags, pretending not to mind his monstrous beast - who at that moment was encircling its master, frenziedly yapping, enraging him further, causing him to stumble, his foot to shoot out from beneath him and -

Whoomp

Dear *God.*

One minute Reggie was before me, the next he was over the side of the cliff.

A quiver of nausea constricted my stomach.

I stood there frozen into immobility, my thoughts running in all directions.

There was a time when I thought my whole life would be torn up by the roots should...should anything happen to Reggie, anything really severing...like...like death or desertion or...or his having a serious illness...or...even his being gay.

I would have been done for, I used to think.

Down into the single life I would sink, and - because Reggie was less than forty then - I would be unpleasantly short of money into the bargain.

But how awful to entertain such thoughts, and the roaring waters at that moment closing over Reggie's head.

Shocked at myself, horror-struck, I plumped down onto my knees.

And my shock and my horror became tremendous when I realised that I was somehow, apart from being shocked and horror-struck, weirdly shot through with a feeling that was not disagreeable.

But no. Impossible.

It was...distress...that made me think like this.

Calm yourself, Sadie. Calm.

I took a deep steadying breath, crawled for a moment, then onto my stomach before peeping over the edge of the cliff.

And there Reggie was, some seven feet below having managed by some miracle - or perhaps his army training - to grab hold of the root of a tree.

"The hell are you at?" His breath was coming fast. "Gimme a hand here - "

I continued to stare with a kind of clinical curiosity.

How ox-like his eyes, I couldn't help thinking. How heated his forehead.

All that anger coming to the surface.

And oh dear, the poor old thing was losing his hair.

Funny, I hadn't noticed that before.

Poor Reggie, who'd been handsome once, striking in his uniform, with his scalp showing pink through his grizzly hair.

Still, though, a bully who'd put his foot down with a bang that echoed along the corridors of twenty-five years.

To think of the rules and regulations.

Years of them. Decades.

"What are you *doing*?" Reggie looked up in stunned incredulity. "Get the dog leash, can't you."

I cleared my throat. "You seem to have lost your glasses, dear. Wouldn't mind you only got them the other day."

Unprepared for such a response, Reggie let rip with a swear word. An amazingly coarse and vulgar word. But then, he'd have heard it in the army, so I couldn't really blame him. Still, though, to speak like that to a lady.

My eyes narrowed.

My lips tightened over my teeth.

Was it his consciousness that I wasn't in fact a lady that made him imagine he could treat me like that?

"Throw me down his leash. You hear me…call the dog."

My calm was unnerving him, my cold unimpassioned interest. But I couldn't help it. Such a situation. Me on top, as it were, for once in my life.

Dear dear dear. The mills of justice starting to grind.

"Do as I *say* - "

"You know very well I'm afraid of the dog."

Reggie was speechless, alarmed for my sanity.

"And anyway he's gone."

I backed from the cliff edge to where the bags were, and began to rummage.

Only a week ago I'd bought a clothesline...if I had it now...I could...tie one end around me...drop the other down...and straining backwards, haul him up.

"Sadie - the hell are you at?"

I came back to the cliff edge and once again got down on my knees.

Reggie, meanwhile, was scrabbling for a foothold, his face more congested than ever. He looked up at me, fire in his eyes.

"You don't imagine, do you, I can stay like this forever?"

The tree root creaked. A shower of dirt spattered his face.

"*Sa*die - " The fear in his voice was palpable. "The *belt* of your coat. Throw it down to me. Quick."

"I...don't have a belt. That's my green coat, Reggie."

"I am not believing this."

"Do you want me to...look around for...a branch or something? Or how about...I take my cardigan off? Only thing is the sleeves are short and I don't think - "

My voice trailed off.

I once again peeped over the edge.

And as Reggie carried on swearing and threatening and bellowing out orders, a strange feeling came over me.

A dreamy remoteness.

Reggie's voice seemed far away.

And I wasn't seeing him. Not really.

Nor did I see the sea, the cliff edge rising in a sheer steep face, spume, rocks jutting up from the billowing waves.

No.

None of these.

What I saw was my sitting room, curtains drawn against the night, my coal fire throwing a warm glow on the fender, a rug I was going to buy with a tabby and not a dog stretched across it, my wing chair, a reading lamp, myself with a glass of Chablis in one hand, a remote control in the other and -

"Saa-deee?"

My eyes focused. Yet a strange light had flooded me and I felt a little dizzy.

"Yes, dear?"

Reggie was breathing with controlled violence while running the whole proverbial gamut from swearing to whimpering, to bargaining, to pleading and back to swearing again.

Then all at once he was silent.

And still.

Strangely still.

I craned my neck and saw to my surprise he'd gained a foothold.

I scrambled to my feet, for now he was finding a handhold too.

With a queer acceleration of my pulse, I backed from the cliff edge, a whole host of conflicting emotions swirling about inside me, chief among them -

Panic.

In the breeze - so much cooler now - my scarf beat out around her ears.

My scarf.

I hadn't thought of my scarf, a remnant I'd bought to cover a bedside table.

Were I to take it off, knot it, and pass it down, I could fairly easily haul him up, but -

I once again peeped over the edge - at the root of the tree, and Reggie's grip which showed no sign of letting up. Stout he might be but Reggie was fit.

And what with a foothold…clawing with his other hand…breath jagged in his throat…it wasn't altogether impossible that -

"You *whore*."

Hearing him pant and curse and bully, remembering my bumps and my mother's disdain, all the blood of all the McTaggarts from time immemorial and properly sensitive to humiliation, abruptly surged within me.

So that - No.

I couldn't *wouldn't* allow it to happen.

Anger, fear, anxiety, dread, thoughts of God and

retribution all swirled about furiously together inside me as I looked down over the face of the cliff and gazed at Reggie who, for his part, was gazing up at me. But through the anger, fear, anxiety, dread, thoughts of God and retribution, one great thought pushed the others aside and shot to the top of the welter: my life was worth nothing <u>should Reggie make it up.</u>

So that what I was about to do, I thought, my head in a roar, was nothing other than self defence.

Yes.

I had to consider my welfare now.

With my eye on the tree root, and the bald spot on Reggie's head, I reached for another bag - the one with the carefully parted bottles - and from it plucked the olive oil.

I hurriedly screwed off its lid.

"WhatAreYou<u>D</u>oing?"

Reggie was staring, his mouth ringed, eyes narrowed with suspicion.

"I am talking to you. Whatareyoudoing?"

Trembling in every limb, lips parted, ears ringing, I lay on my belly again. And holding out the bottle, managed somehow to choke out the words.

"I'm very sorry, Reggie - "

"Hang on, what's this? What-are-you-at?"

"I am letting you down, Reggie. That is - I'm...putting you down`.

"What are you *talking* about?" Reggie's voice was a hamster squeak of horror. "Sadie, what have you got in that bottle?"

"Olive oil. And what I'm talking is business," I said, my voice climbing over his for he'd started to shriek. "Something I would have done a long time ago...only I...I didn't have the courage. Or the opportunity."

"Sadie girl, listen to me - you're upset...not yourself. Get me up now and I give you my word - "

"No, Reggie. You are not a man to keep your

word. Not a man to ever change."

Reggie scrabbled.

He climbed an inch, fell back a little, climbed another inch.

"Listen now. You try to harm me you'll not get away with it. You'll spend the rest of your days behind bars. The police will - "

"I'm sorry, Reggie," I interrupted. "But...you've put me in the position of having to do this."

And with that, I turned the bottle over and let the liquid drip, directly onto Reggie's hands.

"OhmyGod - "

Reggie's eyes and mouth were three round O's of horror for the oil was oozing between his fingers and slowly trickling down his wrists.

"Sadie…no…godammit...Sa - deeeee - "

I rose on one elbow, lidded the bottle, and chucked it over the cliff.

It landed on the rocks at the same time as Reggie.

There followed an eerie silence.

Then, as I got to my feet, "May his soul, and the souls of the faithful departed," I murmured, for the echo of his voice was still in the air. "Through the mercy of God - your God, Reggie, rest in peace."

I rounded off on a husk. "Amen," and stood there looking out to sea, until at last my pulse rate settled.

I would need to go back, talk to the authorities.

Shouldn't have too much trouble.

"Should I, mother?" I said, as I closed my eyes, and filled my lungs with the briny air.

"The dog," I would say, "Dragging him towards the cliff edge. Bit of a brute, amazingly strong, causing poor Reggie to stumble."

And thinking of the dog, I had a quick look over my shoulder.

Not finding him, I thought to leave at once, but...a shame to be indoors on such a day. With a smile that was half-sorrow, half-relief, I lowered myself onto the grass, and leaning across, once again took a hold of my bags.

"Bright citrus," the label on the Chablis declared. "Tropical fruit and mineral notes enliven our Chardonnay's crisp, balanced - "

Chardonnay?

Now, what was it made me think I had bought myself Chablis?

With a slow shake of my head, I uncapped the bottle and brought it to my lips.

Hmmm. Refreshing.

And now for the Fruit and Nut, a sort of little picnic.

"Mother?"

I smiled at a seagull that was hovering above me.

"A shame you aren't here, because really, it's turning out a wonderful day."

Tale of Terry Turkey

The name is Terry turkey
And it's the last week of December
And I bin getting extra grub
Ever since November

I'm sorta getting bad vibrations -
SOMETHIN'S GOIN' ON
Someone mentioned turkey giblets
But could be I heard wrong

I was chatting up this chicken
About this time last year
And when I left her coop at dawn
There was no turkeys anywhere

So. I can't help bein' suspicious
How could they disappear?
And I have this awful hunch
It could occur *this* year

Now I've warned the other turkeys
That they're dangerously fat
But they're so engrossed with gobbling
That they haven't time to chat

Well I'm elopin' with my chicken
(Like, she's in the fam'ly way)
But we'll be back, ye needn't worry
Long after Christmas Day

Might pick this farm again
Dunno - it all depends
But I'm certain I'll not see again
Me poor ole turkey friends

Terry - 11

Yeah, me, Terry Turkey
And I'm pushin' on in years
Last year I was full a life
This year I'm in tears

See I'd married this nice chicken
(she being in the fam'ly way)
But last week by chance I caught her
With this young cock in the hay

And she didn't bat an eye
For the kids she couldn't care
I'd sent her out there as a spy
To see they'd never disappear

For - every single Christmas
For as long as I remember
Every bloody turkey
Disappears around December

Well. I'm packing off the kids
To a hideout on the farm
To me ole flame (Tilly Turkey)
An' she'll save 'em all from harm

But as for me - I'm done.
I've lost me chicken an' me pride
So I'll hang around this Christmas
It's the same as suicide!

Terry - 111

Well here I am back
Terry Turkey once again
This year I'm ecstatic
For I've found a nice new hen
See, I'd hung around last Christmas

Having lost the wife (and pride)
She's absconded with this cock
So I was bent on suicide

But they gave her to a convent
And though it's callous using puns
I'm somehow sorta tickled
Just to think she's in the nuns

But, aye, the kids have all been saved
An' now everything's the same
Apart from certain extra duties
Towards Tilly, me ole flame

And so the grandkids come to see me
An' the greatgrandkids as well
An' when they all start gabblin'
The girlfriend kicks up hell

I'm retired at last all happy
An' I've nothing left to fear
Since I put the rumour out about
The salmonella scare.

Trust Me, I am a Midwife

Nothing to worry about, my dear Mrs al-Majid.

Baby is absolutely fine. Believe me, in all Al-Awja not a finer child.

A little blue, perhaps, but that is all.

And see, just what you hoped for - a boy. Earth brown eyes, tar black hair.

And hear that cry? Not a cry, a *squall.*

Lungs of a leader.

Now now, dear, no tears. Unless, of course, tears of joy.

That, I will permit.

One should not be sad this balmy April morning, sheep grazing high on the mountain, birds singing outside your door.

Oh, I agree, my friend, I agree, terrible to think he shall not know his father. But what can one do when men disappear? We are helpless.

Hush now, hush.

One must keep faith and trust in God but...gone to his Maker, they say, and best to believe it. Poor man, never did anyone any harm. Quietly herding his sheep. A good man, too, for all that he was given to grumbling, and struck you, you tell me, once or twice.

Well, all that is in the past. You have family. You have friends. The support of all the *al-Begat*. No better tribe in all Iraq. What am I saying - in all the world.

But look, do you know what your cousins are thinking? In time you must remarry.

Yes, I know, I know, I could not have chosen a worse occasion to propose it. You are weary, and baby has yet to be put to the breast.

But these are tough times, my dear. One has to look ahead.

To marry again would give your boy a better chance.

How do you know that with a little help - a father figure to guide him - he might not rise to be someone of note - wielding influence on the world's great stage?

Come now, smile.

That's better.

And so, you have chosen a name?

Oh. How nice.

And you know of course what it means? *One Who Confronts.*

Nothing, but *nothing*, could better suit your noisy boy.

Saddam. To be followed up with...Hussein?

A good name. Yes, a manly name.

Easy to remember, and trips off the tongue.

Arrangement in White

"You can't do that."

"Says who?"

"He's on medication. I'm telling you now he could die."

With hounds on my heels, and a shrill voice ringing in my ears, I boldly went where no woman had gone before: down a warren of corridors pushing the wheelchair I'd found in a closet, past Nurse Ratched and out - *out* - into freedom and the stinging freshness of a cold December day.

Bundling my father into the Clio, Ratched leaned towards me expressing in an immense number of words her intention to report me to higher authorities.

"I think you should." I glanced at her over my shoulder. "And when they send for me shall I show them the images I've stored in my iPhone?"

This reduced her to silence as nothing else could.

I stared at her without expression as I slammed the passenger door and handed over the far from fragrant wheelchair.

Minutes later I was on my way and following the

road sign for Castledoran.

For a mile or so I didn't speak.

Now and then I would glance at Father only to find him glancing at me. Coming into a village, he touched a hand to the steering wheel, obliging me to look at him.

"They'll get over themselves." I metered the words out slowly for his hearing aid, I found, did not have a battery. "And who knows, might even get their act together."

Father turned away as though to assimilate this complicated wad of information. I had found him in the shadiest room in the nursing home, the air tainted with the smell of the commode, his radio missing, his water jug out of reach.

But it was the remains of his lunch that sent the blood pounding up to my forehead – spaghetti hoops and buttered bread. A good thing, I thought, they hadn't known I was going to call.

"You're coming home," I said, as I turned the windscreen wipers on, for the first frail snowflakes were sifting through the air. "And staying home. The kids and James can hardly wait. And Da," I added, "wait till you see this new place."

For a moment he watched the passing scene – hedgerows, fields, and leafless trees - then fixed his gaze on me again.

"We're through with London," I carried on, on a spuriously jolly note. "No more going back. Fine for your sons but not for me."

His slow, half-hidden smile was Father's answer to that, for speech was a struggle ever since he'd had the stroke. And as I boggled along the country roads, the snowflakes - swirling down from a leaden sky - brought back with a piercing clarity, ringing across the years, childhood memories - a warm nostalgic tide that threatened to engulf me.

"Hey." I forced a smile. "I don't suppose you remember my hat - you know, the one we wrangled over? It never snows but I think of it."

It was a small white hat that called to me from the window of Flanagan's, a drapery store in Castledoran. More than anything in the world I had coveted that hat, an arrangement in white - velvet, elastic, streamers and bows, and designed to go with nothing so much as Confirmation clothes.

I'd pointed it out to Father, who was bandy-legged under the weight of a sack of potatoes.

"Thirty-five bob? For a snowball like that? Can you hear yourself - thirty-five *shillings*?"

Pale with outrage, he set down his burden the better to remind me that he was by himself with five mouths to feed, and after shelling out for my "costume", my shoes, and my fancy bag, it had to be *No. Sorry. He couldn't afford that extra fal-lal.*

But that extra fal-lal was all I had wanted.

"Price of a leg a lamb," bawled Father, hoiking up his bag again. "Sack a spuds, and a stone of flour."

I turned on him in a kind of blaze.

"If you did without the lamb you could buy me the hat."

"And what," cut in Father, turning away to acknowledge the greeting of a passerby, "is wrong with the cap your granny knit you?"

"It's a hat I want, not a cap. A hat like Connie Rattigan has."

Connie was a friend who invited me to her home every Friday after school.

She lived with her parents above their shop on the

prosperous side of Castledoran. It was a pawnshop - a rambling end-of-block edifice full of quaint alcoves, odd little steps leading up and down to various closets, a storeroom here, a lavatory there, arches, narrow passages branching this way and that into rooms that were filled to bursting with junk.

On days when he wasn't busy, Rattigan would permit us to rummage through his wares. "And while you're at it -" He would open a drawer and throw me a chamois. "Might as well make yourself useful."

A ferret of a man, there hung about the pawnbroker a peculiar smell as of one who rarely changed his clothes. Although not much taller than myself, with stringy hair and stumps for teeth, his every word in my direction was honed with superiority, meant to slice me thin.

"How many brothers did you say you had? Three, begod. And how do ye fit in that little house?"

With all my anguished soul I envied Connie Rattigan, for although her father was a well-known miser, she had everything in the way of worldly goods - a latest model bicycle, a wardrobe full of fancy clothes, a poodle, a summer house in Connemara and - over and above all that - a mother. A woman of stupendous bulk to be sure, one with a peculiar goose-like waddle and a voice more afflicting than her husband's - but yet a mother.

Mine - a soft-voiced, long-limbed beauty - had died the summer before "*after a brief illness borne with fortitude*".

We'd never heard of pancreatic cancer, but it swept her away in the space of a month. This forced Father to leave his job, for no other relative - least of all grandma - was prepared to deal with teenage boys.

That first terrible Christmas, Father's mother came up from Limerick, bringing with her Christmas cheer. Lips pursed, arms akimbo, she wandered from room to room, before returning to the kitchen her eyes dark and glittering in her grey-white face.

She waited till Father had left off gumming an envelope then, "No offence, Dan," she said, looking up at her son from navel height, "but I never saw such a sty in my life."

Holding out her hand for the pen Father hastened to put in it, she grabbed an envelope, drew up a list, dispatched us all on various missions, and by noon the following day had reduced the chaos to order.

On the eve of Christmas Eve, unable to sleep because of grandma snoring, I stole down the stairs to find Father before the fire, eyes fixed on a picture which hung above the mantle clock. It was a black and white photo of my twenty-something mother, enlivened by the beauty of its frame. Tortoiseshell in a fern-and-floral decor, it was a gift from her future husband on the occasion of their engagement. And here he now was, his first Christmas without his wife, transfixed before her image, his lips drawn back in an agonised spasm.

I backed from the crack in the door, and returned to my bed, tightly clenching my teeth to keep the tears from falling down.

Christmas segued into New Year, and Grandma took off to everyone's relief. Time dragged and the weather was bad, but I found in the face of school and other preoccupations that I was slowly getting over Mother.

Then came the month of May, and I yearned to see her again.

"Where are you?" I glared at the tortoiseshell frame. "Can you see or hear me? I'm making my Confirmation and I want a hat."

I ought to pray, I knew.

But the trouble with praying was that it was one-sided, and with only a fortnight to go before the event, I needed to be sure I was being attended. I had a suspicion neither God nor Mother could hear me, because ever since I saw that hat, I'd done everything a mortal girl could do to raise enough to buy it - running errands for elderly neighbours, selling comics that belonged to my brothers, searching through pockets, even, to my shame, nicking a shilling from Rattigan's till.

And still I didn't have enough.

In desperation I applied to Father once again. An untimely approach, for it was a wet Saturday morning and he was using a ruler to separate two of my brothers who were locked together in mortal combat, kicking at each others' shins.

Nevertheless, I couldn't wait.

"You hear me?" I said. `I want that hat."

Father turned on me, his eyeballs fiery.

"Have words lost all meaning? I can't afford it."

I stared at him in stricken silence.

"Look - " Father sighed. He dropped his head and let it swing. "Surely you know if I could I would buy it?"

Wordlessly, I grabbed my coat and left the kitchen.

Father followed me into the hall, and stood with his back to the door. It was drizzling outside, and high in the tower of the Franciscan friary, the bells of the morning Angelus rang splendidly over the town.

"Where d'you think you are going?"

"To the church."

"What for?"

"To pray," I said, "for a miracle."

At those last three words, uttered on a sob, father kept his eyes on beam with mine, and his lips dropped open in an expression I was to remember for the rest of my life. Turning slowly, he opened the door. I hurried past him without a word.

For what seemed like hours I sat in the church, bargaining with a God.

I would return the shilling to Rattigan's till, I solemnly promised, and the sixpenny bit I had nicked from my father, and would never steal in my life again if He would see fit to grant me my request.

A hat.

"That's all I want through Christ our Lord." I

rounded off on a husk, "Amen", just as something came gently down on my shoulder.

I twisted round, to find our neighbour from down the road flashing her gums at me.

"I hope you said one for me?"

I returned Mrs Mulligan's smile, and was forthwith rewarded - to think I'd doubted the existence of God - by the shiny florin she pressed in my palm.

I stared at this windfall, then at my neighbour, and managed somehow to choke out my thanks.

Alight with hope, I left the church and flew to the other end of town to look again in Flanagan's window. Possible they would accept a deposit, and allow me to have the hat.

Breathless, I crossed the road, narrowly missing the wheels of a van. I drew up outside the draper's, to find that the hat was gone from the window.

It was as though a bucket of water were thrown in my face.

Holding my breath, I entered the shop.

"No more hats." The assistant was gleeful. "How about a crochet cap?"

With tightly compressed lips, I returned to the

house and up to my room, ignoring the aroma wafting from the kitchen.

I resolved, there and then, I would not be making my Confirmation. I would be sick on the day - green from all the chocolates that nine and six would buy me.

"Don't want it," I wailed, when Father called me down for dinner.

"Sausages," he said in a cajoling voice.

But I stayed in my room, heroically brooding.

In the end, a growling stomach forced me downstairs.

Although my brothers were gathered round the table, a pall had descended on the house, as though everyone was holding his breath in fearful curiosity for what would happen next.

What happened next, while it partook of the elements of farce, was also bemusing: Father emerging from the scullery, and hand behind his back, escorting me to the table in the manner of a waiter.

Grandly pulling out my chair.

"Yer majesty," said one of my brothers, which occasioned snorts from the others.

Imposing silence with a finger to his lips, Father

swung his hand around, and set a plate before me. On it was not my dinner, but a box tied up with string.

Drum-like, white.

I stared at it, then at my brothers.

"Yeah, g'wan. Open it up."

With a queer acceleration of my pulse, I undid the string, which Father watched with an expression of affectionate expectancy.

Slowly, I lifted the lid.

And finding within, encased in tissues, the hat I'd so passionately prayed for - a queer feeling came over me. It was a moment that could never be repeated, this lifting of my insufferable disappointment.

I raised the hat from its rustling nest, and held it away from the table.

But I couldn't really see it.

My vision had blurred.

And when I turned to look at Father, I found I couldn't speak, for something had risen and stuck in my throat.

Without a word, I fled from the room.

On the morning of my Confirmation I stood before the mirror positioning my hat this way and that and thinking - as Father exhorted me to hurry - that life was not so bad after all. For here was my big day radiant with sunshine, my brothers behaving, my grandma appearing and angrily presenting me with a prayer book and two crisp ten shilling notes.

In all Castledoran that lovely May morning as I skipped ahead of my family and bounded into the church, there was no happier creature than twelve-year-old me.

It was destined not to last for long.

The following Monday I hurried home from school, took out my purse, and counted my savings. Time to pay off my debts. I returned the sixpence to Father's pocket and was setting aside what was owing to Rattigan, when I raised my head and looked around. Something in the house wasn't right.

My eyes did a quick flight about the kitchen, but nothing appeared out of place. Bemused, I pocketed my purse, found my coat, and made my way across the town.

"Homework," said Rattigan, when I enquired after Connie. "See you on Friday."

Stung by this chilly dismissal, and my thwarted effort to return his coin, I waded my way through an obstacle course of knick-knacks.

Half-way to the door, I halted slightly, continued three steps, then, frowning, turned back.

On an eye level shelf, wedged between a vase and an ornamental clock, was something that had no business being there: a tortoiseshell frame with a fern-and-floral decoration. For how long I stared at it I never knew, but seeing it in Rattigan's shop, I knew a terrible grief, for here was how I had come by my hat.

Turning my head, I gazed at Rattigan, and enquired the price of Mother's frame.

"Twenty-one and six," came the flat, uninterested voice.

With gritted teeth, I dug in my purse and threw out the money.

If Rattigan sensed my contempt, he showed no sign of it. He stretched his neck to re-set it within the circumference of his collar, and as he parcelled the frame, his smile warmed up a fraction.

"Let you come back after tea."

My chin went up a defiant notch as I grabbed the change he was holding out.

"No," I said. "I won't."

"Oh. And why not?"

I ordered myself not to say it. I said it.

"Because you're a rat, Mr Rattigan."

And with that for an exit line, I took to my heels.

I never did go back to the shop, until I heard it was on the market. It is now our guesthouse with airy rooms, open fires, gleaming windows, hanging baskets.

And a ramp at the front to make it easy for Father.

Shackled

"Just as well those two snuffed it," he said. "Because if they didn't, d'you know what would have happened? They'd have gone ahead and set up house. Or, more likely, flat. Yeah, definitely flat. And a grotty one at that, you may be sure."

She thought for a moment then said, "Because of being still in their teens?"

"Aye." He burped softly and stared off into the middle distance. "Y'see, with little in the way of support it would've been a struggle - finding a nest to be constantly making love in. Somewhere where the rellies weren't, in any event. Peace, comfort. D'yeh want any crisps?"

"But, say Romeo didn't snuff it and Juliet hung on, and all went according to plan."

"You mean the warring rellies gave them space?"

"And support."

"They'd have tied the knot, Kirsty my girl, and then guess what - and the same goes for Keats and Fanny Brawne, Heathcliff and Cathy, Cleo and Mark Anthony, and others like them - "

"What?"

"We'd have no sweet poetry, would we? No tears. No love letters for Fanny to read in her field of bluebells."

"No philosophy, huh?"

"Certainly no divine hours leaning over balconies, or howling into graves. Waiter, same again please. And a packet a crisps."

"Right. And so, what brought all this - "

"No sighing or weeping. No gnashing of teeth."

"Yes, but - "

"No conflict. Nothing for your drama departments to get their teeth into."

"Right."

"What we *would* have," he said as he took out his wallet, "in the case of the Romeos, is a squad of kids. Juliet moaning for entirely different reasons. Romeo with a receding hairline and a Pavarotti belly. Try to imagine him, swanning around, forgetting to wash, breaking wind after drinking his bock."

"Well," She pulled a face. "It's what you call getting comfy."

"Call it that if you like, but if you ask me - "

"Okay, Angus. The point of all of this?"

"The point of all of this?' he parroted. He looked away, looked back again. "We'd have lost a lot if those two Italians had made it to eighty."

"So, something to be said for going young, is what you mean?"

"Aye, so long as you're looking your absolute best. Think Marilyn Monroe, The Princess of Wales, JFK, James Dean, River Phoenix, Curt Cobain, Heath Ledger - "

"All went at the right time?"

"We remember them as picturesque. I mean, try to see them at eighty. At ninety. They wouldn't have liked it. Nor would we."

"So what you are basically saying is - "

"You want people to remember you fondly, and with tears in their eyes, go young, go with the bloom of youth on your face."

"And this thing called love?"

"I was getting to that. Nothing, but pure illusion. A cruel trick as someone once said played on us by nature to ensure the propagation of the species."

"Right."

The barman came, set down their drinks and the

packet of crisps.

"What I'm really trying to tell you, Kirsty, is - "

"Yes?"

"That the chemicals that told me four years ago that I was in love with you have, well, fizzled out and uh I have this feeling of you and me being, well, what *you* call comfy and I call shackled." He opened the crisps with a little burst. "We're shackled creatures, Kirsty, do you realise that?"

"Shackled? That what you call being engaged?"

"...the thing that makes me hate meself most is my inability to tell you. Until now. With four pints of Harp inside me, that - that there is someone else. Someone I *really* love. And well, if you could gimme back my ring and uh try and imagine the pair of us at eighty, Isobel and meself. Sans teeth, sans taste, sans eyes, sans - the fuck, my wallet. Where is it? Kirsty - my car keys. Hey, come back here. Waiter - could you stop that woman. Kirsty, god*damn*."

Civilising Savages

Hey, you with the small metal head
And them spiky things over your eyes
My name is Brother Alphonsus
Sorry, did I give you a surprise?

Look, I'm here to check your persuasion
Are you Protestants, Catholics or Jews?
Maybe you're Muslims or Mormons?
Well, look, I'm here to give the Good News

Have you ever had impure thoughts?
Plundered another guy's treasure?
Done anything you can think of at all
That'd give you unwarranted pleasure?

Has anyone mentioned your baptism?
For a start it's an absolute must
Oh begod now, that poses a problem
You couldn't get wet or you'd rust…

And so, where do ye go for confessions?
You realise that you're not wearing clothes?
Only savages go around naked
With all their contraptions exposed

Do you ever be thinking of women?
Do you drink till ye fall on your face?
Have ye heard that you'll sizzle in hell
If you're not in the right state a grace?

Do you know that you're primitive beings?
Though you've never had bloodshed or worse
Never had fighting or brawling
But still I don't give a curse

Would ye hurry and kneel at me feet
Don't stand there like dustbins and mope
I'll baptise you with Three-in-One oil
Then I'll have to report to the Pope.

Double Buggy

I push this double buggy
Every summer up this hill
Kid before and after me -
Wish I took the pill

Oh now the double buggy
Is zoomin' down the hill
Five of us are on it
Sleigh ride, if you will

This road is gettin' narrow
Would you push ahead there, Bill
Never have this torment
If I'd gone and took the pill

Ah good, we're near the sea
And it's gettin' warm and muggy
Never would a made it now
Without the double buggy

Grr. The oldest one is missing
He must be on that hill
Come down you pup, I'll flake you
Oh, I wish I took the pill

Splashing in the water
With the twins Irene and Jill
To think I'd not have had them
If I'd gone and took the pill

Manoeuvring the buggy home
It takes a bit a skill
Yet everyone looks angry
Yeah, I should of took the pill

I'm contented when they're happy
When they roar I've had my fill
And I nag me poor old husband
That I wish I took the pill

Here's to you, Mrs R

"She ought to be airlifted, Dr Griffin."

A shiver of horror passed over Tim.

Here he was, a newly minted doctor in a village in the middle of nowhere, snowed in at four in the morning. Lines down, lights out. The patient too far gone to go to hospital.

"Deep breath, Mrs Robinson. Hold the torch up, nurse. That's it, now... *push*!"

Mrs Robinson pushed. Nothing happened.

She pushed again.

And again.

A minute passed. Ten. Fifteen.

Still nothing.

"Okay. I'm going to give you a little help."

"She ought to be airlifted, Dr Griffin."

Tim sighed, for the midwife was watching in stark disapproval as he slewed away to take up the forceps. Propped against the wall, his eyes fixed on Tim, was Mrs Robinson's husband. About them, the room lay in disarray - sheets, towels, basins, instruments.

Impaled by its point in the lino was the hypodermic syringe Tim had used the moment before.

"Now then," said Tim, as a dew of sweat formed on his brow. "This may pinch a little..."

"Ahhhh..."

"She ought to be airlifted, Dr Griffin."

"Sorry. Take a rest now, Mrs R. You're being very brave."

Time dragged. Mrs Robinson writhed.

"All right, then. A deep breath. Now – *push*."

Tim's body, heated by his exertions, suddenly chilled. For the patient seemed to have given up.

"One push, Mrs Robinson, and it's all celebrations, child in your arms, pain forgotten."

"She ought to be airlifted, Dr Griffin."

Tim closed his eyes in a gesture of patience, got down to it dregs, opened them to say, "You can do it, Mrs Robinson. Come, now. One last big push."

A wail arose, not from the patient but her husband who fled the room, unable to endure any more. Hardly had the door closed behind him than the child popped into the world.

"Well done, Mrs R. Well done, well done. A daughter."

Dawn was breaking by the time that Tim struck out

for home, picking his steps because of the snow. On his lips was a smile, under his arm the bottle of port the sheepish Mr Robinson plucked out of a cupboard. Being Saturday, he had stayed to raise a glass and wish the family well. Back in his apartment, he fell into bed.

The phone rang.

"Dr Griffin?"

It was Lorcan of Mucky Malone's letting him know that Margaret the midwife slipped on the ice outside his pub.

"Looks to be concussed. Any suggestions?"

Tim sat up, his lip twisting.

"Airlifting," he intoned. "And into hospital. Gimme a minute and I'll organise it."

Merry Christmas God Bless You

Deck the Halls with boughs of holly
Carol singers very jolly
Handed out 10p
Carol singers stare at me
Forked out 5p more
Singers verge upon my door
'Tis the season to be jolly
Walloped me with boughs of holly.

Song of Summer

Monday 15th July.

The day I had planned to run away.

Dawn. House shrouded in silence. Only sounds the pipe of a bird, snores from the room beyond the kitchen, and the crowing of a cock in the distance.

I lay on my side, groping my way through thick waves of torpor.

Ungluing an eye, I looked around the shadowy room, thinking that this time tomorrow I would be back in my own room, a bed to myself, a carpeted floor, window facing the other way.

I should have left earlier, I thought, as I half turned over and considered my bedmate. Lost to the world was ten-year-old Cait as she lay on her back, hair tousled, lips parted, her slight, regular breathing like nothing so much as a finger sliding across a page and - time to get up.

Up, up, I exhorted myself. Yet although I half rose from my pillow, I couldn't bring myself to leave the bed.   My limbs were creeping with heaviness and warmth.

I dropped down heavily on the pillow again. Two hours later I woke to the realisation I had missed the early morning bus.

But no matter. The next one left in three hours' time. The problem was how to reach it without being seen.

Outrageous, I knew, to be running away. A wholly ungrateful practice. Yet for days on end I had considered nothing except the acuteness of the joy of doing it.

I knew, of course, I would be in for it when I stepped off the bus at the other end, and Mother clocked me from behind the curtain coming up the street towards the house, a smile on my face, a shoulder pulled down by the weight of my suitcase.

I had a clear vision of her letting go of the curtain, flinging open the door, and looking holes through me.

"What's this? Why-didn't-you-let-me-know-you-were-coming?"

And my smile - contracting by a yard or two - would beg for one in return. Knowing Mother, she wouldn't oblige. Which would make it all the harder for me to explain why it was I had run away: boredom. Sheer and unrelieved.

To complain of such a thing - I who had used it as an excuse to get away - would be to place myself beyond the reaches of mercy. For, ever since the start of summer, I had pleaded to be let off to Curnagopple where I would be nothing if not a blessing to my relatives.

"Will you listen to her," said Mother, on a sudden loud laugh.

I looked at her. "What?"

Her laugh fell away. "You can stay here and be a blessing to me."

Terrible, I said, to have no one to turn to. No brother to fight your corner, no sister. Not even a father.

"Tough," said Mother, handing me a broom and pointing to crumbs I had dropped on the floor.

I opened up further stops, increasing the volume of my dirge.

I didn't even have a friend.

Everyone who was anyone had gone away. I was bored with nothing to do except servant's work in a miserable house for no reward. I was something out of Dickens. Why couldn't I go to Curnagopple?

Because, said Mother, in a tone of voice that said

she was running out of patience, there was no room for me at Curnagopple. Four youngsters in a tiny cottage, nothing for Rosie but extra work. And talking of which, she added, over what I was about to let loose on her, now I was fifteen I ought to have a summer job.

I dropped the broom and made for the door, but not before sounding one last shameful chord.

"If you gave a damn for me you'd let me go."

That evening, Mother wrote to them at Curnagopple, and five days later I was dispatched with the injunction I was to eat whatever was set before me, be an example to the cousins, clear off to bed when given the nod, steer clear of the neighbours' sons, and never go anywhere near a well.

And so, like a war child with my labelled suitcase and pocketful of coins, she marched me to the bus stop, and instructed the driver as to where to let me off.

Three hours later I was met by my aunt in the village of Glebe, then taken by taxi the two and a half

miles to the outreaches of Co Clare.

But no sooner had I entered the farmhouse than I began to have misgivings.

There were things I had overlooked: no transport, no running water, no television. I would have to share a bed. No sweetshop except in Glebe. No cinema to go to on days when it rained.

On the other hand, I reminded myself, my cousins were glad to see me. Being a townie, I was a kind of providence to them, telling them stories more colourful perhaps than accurate, saving them from endless hours of dullness and furnishing their drab country lives with mystery and romance.

We could become, I told them, the Curnagopple Famous Five, enjoying the sort of adventures Enid Blyton only imagined - midnight feasts with cakes and jam, secret meetings in hay lofts, forays in search of treasure, picnics in the ruins of the Tully Castle a mile or two down the road.

Oh yes, the summer of '64 would be the one to hang on the wall.

And as I beamed at my cousins who were gathered around me that first sunny afternoon, waiting for me to open my suitcase, the magic word, freedom, rang in my ears. Released from the dullness of home and the heavy harness that was school, the next six weeks lay before me like a blessing.

But before the evening was out, the sun disappeared, and a blanket of cloud hung over the countryside and there remained for the next five days. The feeling was one of being smothered. Next came the rain, soft and persistent, hardly more than a mist and peculiar to that much-soaked corner of Ireland.

The lanes became chocolate.

The gardens and fields were amazingly green.

The leaves of every tree glistened with wet.

The roses and nasturtiums were goblets of water.

And as I sat inside the window looking out at the sodden landscape, I grimly dwelt on the gulf that seemed to be fixed between life in books and life as it was really was.

Then, just as I was thinking of home again, the sun came out from behind the clouds, our moods lifted, and the fun at last began: forays into orchards that weren't ours, hide and seek in fields of corn, rides on a donkey that nobody owned, a prowl around the grounds of the ancient Tully Castle.

But there was no treasure to be found, no scientists needing our help, no pirates to stalk, no shipwreck to look for. And as the days dragged by and the first delight of leading the way was blunted by repetition, I began to yearn for home again. But how to leave without estranging the family? My brain, after working at top speed in manufacturing excuses could come up with nothing more riveting than, "I want to go home."

But preoccupied by a dozen crosses sent to try her - dentures that didn't fit, a jug that slipped from her hands and shattered into smithereens, chickens reported missing - aunt Rosie shooed me away.

I tried again the following day, but she was baking and not lightly to be approached.

On the third day, I followed her into the hen house.

"Yerra," she said, when finally I got the message through, "you can't go home till I fatten you up."

My thoughts began to move at a great pace and suddenly were lit up by a flare of rebelliousness. This was imprisonment. I wouldn't stand for it.

If they wouldn't let me go, I would up and run away. It would constitute a genuine adventure which, although certain to land me in trouble, would raise me up in my cousins' eyes.

And so, here at last the morning was, a morning like all the others - daylight filtering through the moth-eaten curtains, hens going `buck-buck` on the manure heap outside the window, magpies squabbling below in the orchard, Rosie in the kitchen placidly churning, gravel popping under the tyres I knew to be the postman's bike.

I rolled over in the bed, causing it to creak and Cait to wake. She stared at me out of two accusing blue eyes then drifted off to sleep again.

9:05 my wristwatch said.

The bus would be leaving at noon and the thought of the walk to Glebe was not a little daunting. What if it rained? Or I couldn't manage my suitcase? What if I missed the bus? Was there a later one? Did I have enough money to stay in lodgings? What if Rosie came lepping after me? And how would I deal with her wrath?

Although my courage began to ebb, it was too late now to change my mind: my hand was on the plough and there was no turning back.

With a sidelong glance at Cait, I slid from the bed, dressed, and tiptoed into the kitchen. Rosie had left off churning and was over by the window staring out at nothing.

One hand held a letter, the other was pressed to her mouth which was working. I asked if anything was the matter.

She turned and looked at me as though from an immense distance.

Her eyes were vacant.

I was about to say something when my ears picked up the crunch of footsteps over gravel. Moments later Uncle Jim was in the kitchen.

"God save all here," he said insincerely, before setting down his buckets which brimmed with frothing milk. Alerted by the silence, he nudged his glasses up his nose then looked from one of us to the other.

In my earliest memory, Jim McNamara is in our parlour, extending a hand to my mother, and in a hushed and solemn voice telling her he is sorry for her trouble.

Narrow face, hook nose.

Dome of forehead, penny glasses.

And even at six I am thinking how strange it is that Pope Pius XII should be living on a farm instead of in a church.

"What's up?" Jim's eyes were on the letter. "Nothing bad I hope?"

Rosie came back to buzzing life. "Yanks," she said. "That pair, Ted and Charlie."

"What about them?" said Jim, his mouth ringed with sudden anxiety.

"What about them?" said Rosie, as she leaned forward to sneer at Jim with indescribable malice. "They're on their way over, *that's* what's about them. You will see them this day week, the curse of Cromwell."

It was the start of an anti-Yank jeremiad which seemed justified when I saw what had to be done: the cottage whitewashed inside and out, the manure heap spirited away to the other end of the farm, lace curtains taken down, new ones put in their place, the dresser painted along with the door, chairs barrowed from the neighbours because forms on either side of the table

would only be letting you down.

Goes without saying, I put off running away, and pitched in with my cousins.

Directed by Rosie, we washed and polished, swept and dusted, fetched and carried.

Charged with purpose, we moved about briskly, toiling from dawn until dusk.

Although the chores seemed never-ending, our energy was boundless, unlike poor Rosie who walked a tightrope of nervous tension.

"What did I do to deserve this?"

Over and over she would bewail her lot and wish that people would stay in their own homes and not place others in such terrible situations.

"But shure they're only passing through," said the neighbour who spirited our forms away and replaced them with her fancy chairs. "And what are they but a pair of lads."

Rosie's New World nephews last hit Ireland in 1960.

It didn't help that they were officers-in-training at the same Military Academy attended once by President Eisenhower, that they hailed from a home in
the leafy suburbs, that their standard answer to everything was *Wow, how about that,* that they had at their disposal items you only saw in the cinema or read about in magazines - cars, refrigerators, percolators, showers, tvs, phones that extended into other rooms.

That Rosie's sister should occupy a mansion in a land of milk and honey, while she churned butter in a cottage that hadn't as much as running water - was a trial not to be borne.

Although sorry for Rosie's troubles, and wishing she were richer, there was no denying that this great upheaval gave kick to a life which was otherwise flat.

"They're here, Ma. The Yanks are here."

D-Day had come at last.

Since early morning cousin Kevin had stationed himself in the branches of the elm tree which stood by the front gate and from which he could command the road and be the first to spot our visitors.

Hearing his Comanche yell, we rushed from the house to find him waving to us from the running board of a gleaming black Morris Minor which was trundling up the potholed incline.

Kevin jumped off as it drew to a stop at the top of the drive.

The doors opened and Stewart Granger and Buddy Holly stood there. So different were they from the sorts of people we were used to I suddenly realised why Rosie had fretted. Tall, rangy, relaxed and tanned, they made us look and feel what we really were - an uneasy, pale-faced, dingy lot. And yet, although you could imagine them sailing through life without a care in the world - porters, taxi drivers and waiters rushing to be of service to them - they seemed oddly shy.

"Hi."

A moment's awkward silence was followed by a flurry of greetings, smiles, kisses, bear hugs. Then "Hey?" as Buddy drew back, and turned the full light of his glasses on each of us in turn. "You guys going somewhere?"

A query that brought out blotches on Rosie's neck. For we were standing before the cottage like soldiers guarding a tomb, washed, coiffed, and buttoned up in our Sunday best.

But although embarrassed by the question, acutely aware that compared to ourselves her nephews were casually dressed - slacks, sandals, open neck shirts - Rosie quickly rallied. Mumbling something about Holy Days and Mass, she shooed the dog away and motioned us into the kitchen.

But her troubles were far from over, for the Yanks on being offered a drink, mildly enquired if there was any chance of a cup of coffee - filtered, if she had it.

Rosie froze, the teapot suspended motionless in her hand. And when, in a tight voice she declared that her coffee pot was broken, I honked.

Rosie's eyes met mine fiercely, but she carried on heroically pressing tea and soda bread on her visitors, while keeping up a flow of conversation.

Lunch was barely over when Rosie, in answer to a long dissertation on the American way of life smiled hugely and said, "That's groovy."

At the absurdity of such a word falling from Rosie's lips I struggled and triumphed over a snort. But when, after a brief tour around the farm, Buddy enquired which way to the bathroom, I giggled.

Rosie looked at me, knives in her eyes.

How she conveyed to them that the bathroom was outdoors I could never afterwards remember. What I do recall is the long sigh of relief which exhaled from her when the Yanks announced it was time to press on - there were others they wanted to see.

The last glimmer of the Morris Minor having vanished round the bend in the drive, stays were loosened, dentures removed, shoes kicked off, the table cleared, the men sent back to finish the hay.

Rosie, at ease at last in her baggy clothes, ordered us girls to grab a chair apiece and follow her up to the neighbours'.

I hadn't expected to have misbehaved the way I did and not hear about it. But, expansive in her happiness, Rosie had no thought for anything except to get back to the way she had been. The relief of being freed sooner than she had expected produced a liveliness in her she had never shown before.

It would be short-lived.

For, in the distance a small black dot was powering towards us along the boreen.

Disappearing between hedges of fuchsia.

Re-appearing.

Throwing back slicks of light from the afternoon sun.

The nearer it came, the less Rosie had to say.

Suddenly she froze, an animal alerted to danger.

"Is it how ye lost yeer way?" she squawked, when the Morris Minor at last pulled up and Buddy and Stewart opened their doors.

"Not really." Stewart came round the front of the

car and stood alongside his brother. "We're just looking round. But say, where are you guys off to?"

There followed a moment's great hesitation while Rosie ransacked her brain and came up with the perfect lie.

"The neighbours'. They were looking for a loan of my chairs."

"How about that?" Buddy took off his glasses and held them up to the light. "Want us to give you a ride there?"

"Oh, no," Rosie quavered. "They're just around the corner. If it's...Dublin yeer heading for, yeer going the wrong way."

Confronted by this zeal in disposing of them, Buddy's mouth opened and closed. He looked to Stewart who was chewing gum and staring wistfully into the distance.

An awkward silence ensued, then they both took turns to come at Rosie. And clear was it that what they were saying had been carefully rehearsed.

"Know what you got here, Rosie?"

"An air-conditioned country."

"Free of traffic."

"People."

"Exhaust fumes."

"Noise."

Another longer pause, where Stewart moodily kicked up a pebble. Then, with a sideways glance at his brother as though to say, *are you ready*?

"Know what you *don't* have, Rosie?"

"Tenements," said Buddy as he polished his glasses and put them on.

"High rise apartments," continued Stewart.

"Subways."

"Overcrowding."

"Rules."

"Regulations."

"And the damndest thing of all - "

"Being drafted into armies."

At this, a change came over Rosie, who had looked from one to the other like a kitten following a piece of string. Her fingers holding the chair didn't tighten over the rungs. Not a muscle moved, yet she had changed, for in her normal voice - merely stating a fact - she said, "You lads must be tired. Why don't ye stay a night or two?"

The brothers looked at each other, then at Rosie. Was it triumph I saw in their eyes?

"You sure?"

"We don't mind where you put us."

"I'm sure."

Rosie swung round, her face flushed, the leg of her chair clashing with mine.

Placing a hand on the back of my head, she marshalled me forward, and what she said next caused the ground to give way beneath me.

"I'll have one less mouth to feed tomorrow. This wee woman is going home."

A Man Called Wolf

Wolf.

It was a weird name to call him and I wondered about its genesis for there was nothing lupine in his manner, albeit he was scruffy.

I first saw him when he stumbled into the pharmacy and bawled out over the heads of several customers that he needed something for the fleas.

"They nearly lifted me out of the bed last night," caused every head to turn and look at him.

He stood in the doorway grinning inanely, then, with an air, came forward into the shop. A lady in a sheepskin coat gave him a wide berth. Clear was it from his crumpled clothes, his want of grooming, and the sour odour that hung about him, he was a vagrant.

It was September `73 and I was one week into my job - a newly qualified pharmacy technician - and wasn't sure what to do. Then I saw that little, in fact, was expected of me. For, on spotting me behind the counter all important in my new white lab coat, the vagrant moved further into the shop, his dark eyes narrowed. "Howrya," he said as though he'd known me for years. "Go and tell Barney Wolf is here."

At which, Barney, a chemist's assistant, came striding out of the dispensary, a box of flea powder treatment in hand. I half-expected this west of Ireland man, who was given to bouts of contrariness, and who once or twice locked horns with our boss, a thirty-something pharmacist, to quickly dispose of the vagrant then spray the shop with floral scented fresh air spray.

None of it.

"How's it going?" was his opening gambit which surprised not just myself but the lady in the sheepskin coat who looked first at Barney, then at the vagrant before turning round to hand me a prescription.

"Haven't seen you in a while."

This was met with silence, for across the long glass counter, beneath which was a display of Coty perfumes, the vagrant was playing an invisible piano. He was far out at sea, absorbed in something only he could hear.

And the strange thing was that, despite that customers were standing around, Barney was prepared to wait out whatever time it took until the other should get to shore.

Why, I wondered, would he indulge a vagrant?

Who was this man who called himself Wolf?

Who, for that matter, was Barney?

I looked at him. Tall and spare with a natty suit beneath his lab coat, he had more the air of a hospital doctor than assistant to a chemist. You wouldn't dare engage him in idle conversation, for the honour of his company he conferred on none. Your opinions and the affairs of the world outside the shop were matters to him of supreme unimportance.

Yet when it came to the vagrant he was strangely attentive, doling out such items as soap, razor blades, aspirin, and the occasional bottle of Buckfast Tonic Wine with a brisk but friendly air and the assurance he would put the lot on the slate for him.

The slate would be cleared not by the vagrant but by Barney himself, who would call on me to bear witness that the amount owing was being paid in full and that he – that is to say Wolf – had his pride and wouldn't be looking for 'anything off'.

Some months would go by before I would come across the vagrant again. He was shuffling up a side street one cold December afternoon, stopping now and then to examine something in the gutter.

It was the lunch hour and as I stood at the edge of the kerb waiting to cross the road, I saw emerge from the porch of a pub a rather furtive looking Barney. Collar up against the cold, he was looking to where I was looking.

When Wolf was two shops away, Barney slid a treasury note from his wallet, scrunched it and dropped it in the gutter. Then, edging backwards, he waited.

Wolf's approach was painfully slow, but at length he was abreast of the pub. Seeing the note, he stooped to have a closer look, picked it up and smoothed it out.

Although his face showed no expression, his step was lively as he powered back the way he had come.

I stayed where I was until Barney came out of the shadows.

"We were schoolmates," he said, in answer to my stare. "He comes of a respectable Sligo family."

Guardedly, for Barney's mouth was a tight rosette, I commended him for his kindness. For which he rounded on me with a fury.

It wasn't kindness, he intoned. It was duty. If their positions were reversed Wolf - who had once been a gifted pianist affectionately known as Wolfgang and whose real name was Hughes - would certainly do the same for him.

Barney sniffed, no doubt annoyed with himself for opening up as much as he had.

Then, to indicate that the subject was closed, he jerked up his wrist and glared at the time. Three minutes later he was back in the shop.

It was his kingdom which he ruled with an iron fist. He deferred to no one, only Wolf who assumed he had Messianic qualities for, no matter what the complaint - headaches, insomnia, hangover, humming in the ears – Barney had the cure.

That his miracle powders were nothing more potent than crushed up tablets of Vitamin C was testament to Barney's shrewdness and the power of suggestion.

Three years into my job Wolf passed away and Barney talked about retiring.

The pharmacist wouldn't hear of it.

He wheedled, cajoled, dangled every carrot he could think of - part-time work, beefed up salary, extended holidays.

Barney didn't bite. "Why?" he asked. "Why would you bother?"

"Because," replied the pharmacist, "we would all

go flat without you. Besides which, I need someone to be afraid of."

Expiation

For detraction, sloth, gluttony
For gambling all the rent
For stretching truths - backbiting
In a few days I'll repent
For my aggro at the steering wheel
For the car which got a dent
For denying flat to hubby
That I patched it with cement
For warring with the neighbours
For sulking in my tent
For making overt passes
At a handsome colleague gent
For hinting to the colleagues
(When the latter let me down)
That it wasn't for no reason
Syphilis hit the town

Oh I'll fast, atone, abstain, and pray
Down on both knees bent
Make up to all the neighbours
Own up about the gent

No longer be the sybarite

Or wealthy folk resent

I'll be penitent, and faultless

For

....

The first few days of Lent.

Two on a Raft

Don't-do-it. Don't-do-it.

He scurried through the station, heart fluttering to the rhythm of words that had somehow got into his head, an invocation that the more he tried to shake it off, the more firmly entrenched it seemed to become.

But plagued though he was, he was suddenly beset by something worse: a bizarre feeling of not being there.

Connolly Station was at once familiar and utterly strange.

He felt curiously removed, as though a glass wall had come down between him and the rest of the world. Drawing a deep steadying breath, and wishing he were drawing water from his well, he ordered himself not to panic.

He panicked.

The crowds oozed and swayed around him while he stood there, heart rattling, chest heaving, a heavy sense of vertigo threatening to overcome him.

But presently he recovered, and his senses came back to him with a rush.

He carried on, weaving his way in and out among

the commuters, and made it to the train with minutes to spare.

His heartbeats felt less violent now, and an increasing dignity attended his step as he looked about for a place to sit. Towards the rear of the coach he settled himself comfortably in a window seat.

Well, he thought, with a twist of his lip, a table to himself, a broadsheet, and sun spilling into the carriage could only have one meaning: his day was turning round.

He hadn't even luggage to contend with, for his stay in the city had been sweet and brief – just enough time to let them know the die had been cast, and once the legal side of things was sorted, he would pull in with them. Or, more accurately, into their garage.

Tom heaved a sigh that was half-relief, half-regret.

It wasn't the worst arrangement for a widower past his sell-by: the son and his wife on the other side of a load-bearing wall, the hospital down the road should his retina ever detach again, a bus stop round the corner, a row of shops across the green.

What more could a pensioner ask for?

Yet Tom couldn't say he felt good as the train

started off at exactly eleven.

No.

Ever since dawn he'd lain awake on his new single bed in the new remodelled garage and stared up glumly at the new venetian blind on the new velux window, and considered the slab of ice that had somehow lodged in the pit of his stomach, and which even now, as the train was picking up speed, sent cold little shivers running through his veins and up and down his spine.

What was it - anxiety about his uncertain future? Fear of advancing age? Some harking back to his childhood - even the jungle?

Don't-do-it. Don't-do-it.

The rhythm of his heart became the rhythm of the train, and a sudden despondency fell upon Tom as he gazed, unseeing, out the window.

He shouldn't have done it.

No.

A hundred and twenty for a house built of local stone was not enough, even in a recession. True, the eighty-five for his doormat of land was a fair enough offer. But all in all, seventy less than the son had hoped for.

Stupid of him to have allowed that agent to talk him down.

He should have stood his ground and haggled. Or at the very least drawn McAllister's attention to a fact he'd apparently overlooked: that he, Tom, had water rights, what the law referred to as riparian. And, as everyone knew, land with water running through it ought to fetch a decent price.

"Okay to sit here?"

Tom looked up with a swift expectancy.

A backpacker was standing there, a tall young black man who took Tom's raised eyebrows to be an affirmative, settled across from him, and began to toy with one of those gadgets Robbie and the missus carried about.

Was it iPhones they called them?

Amazing the things folks nowadays couldn't seem to do without, thought Tom, as he opened his paper and affected to read. Things considered luxuries by people like himself, and were unknown to his people before him. And not just iPhones and laptops, but ways of life that boggled the mind: extensions to houses that cost as much as the houses themselves.

Holidays to places only convicts ever went to. Surgery to make you look younger. Sports that carried risks like jumping from planes or diving into rapids in little rubber boats. Not that he begrudged folks.

Certainly not Robbie and Anna.

Their jobs demanded a certain lifestyle. And here was something else to truly depress him: he had no idea what their work entailed. Designers of some sort - but of *what*?

"Websites." Robbie had closed his eyes in a gesture of patient endurance. "Want me to go over it again?"

No use, no use.

The thing to do was enrol at a night school in Dublin.

Not alone would it raise his opinion of himself, it would help integrate him when the pair had people over. For how often had he found himself hovering around the edges of things, heroically trying to find a point in any conversation where he could best catch hold and climb on board, as it were.

And failing.

Nothing for it when that occurred but to busy

himself in topping up drinks, before pleading exhaustion with Anna, and slipping away to indulge his morbid talent for solitude.

It was then he yearned for Maggie, his guiding light and other half.

A plain-speaking woman with Scotland in her ancestry, she'd have piloted him through the shoals, positioning herself at the helm of conversation, steering it in interesting directions, always making sure he was on board.

Poor Maggie Cockburn, with that time bomb in her brain. Gone behind the clanking gates of death. Without her, he was rudderless, adrift, no longer at home in the world. And how about that for giving way, chided Tom, his lips tightening over his teeth. The sort of wallowing he despised in others.

An insult to Robbie and Anna.

Had they not been kind to him - giving him all they could in the seven years of his widowerhood - sympathy, time, attention? And now a key to their door? An ungrateful practice surely to imagine that beneath their kindness and cheeriness he could detect a faint little thread of impatience, indifference to his lonely state, and even - dear God, let it not be so - a hint of embarrassment?

"Uh, pardon me."

Tom glanced up as the backpacker sneezed.

American.

And by the looks of him still in his teens. Who was he, Tim idly wondered? Where was he going? Furtively watching the young man's thumbs deftly work his iPhone, Tom called to mind a story he'd heard about a freed slave, Tony Small, who after some American battle or the other had saved the life of Lord Edward Fitzgerald. Imagining he was rewarding Small, Fitz brought him back to Ireland.

What had become of him?

How did he fare in a place so far from what he was used to, and with people so unlike himself he would have roused in them surely the same sort of curiosity the natives of Africa felt when Livingstone walked among them?

And here I am, thought Tom, angst-ridden over a move two hours down the road to my own flesh and blood.

Man up, he ordered himself. *Catch yourself on*.

And yet, as his thoughts dwelt on his little farm and his first winter away from home, he heard again those dreaded words.

Don't-do-it. Don't-do-it.

It was the voice of Maggie's one great friend who owned and ran the Killydoon, a picturesque pub with a quaint half-door and an open fire the whole year round. Terrible to think of her selling up, she who was an institution, and the last feeble thread that bound him to Maggie.

"It's a case of having to." Sarah had studied him with a grave reflectiveness. "I can't afford the upkeep. But *you* don't have to leave here. Are you sure you know what you're doing?"

And Tom, holding his glass out for a refill, felt some sort of disturbing electrical field form around his heart.

"It can be lonely above at the farm. But even if it wasn't -" He pointed to the eye that had given him

trouble. "The old machine is wearing down."

Behind her glasses, Sarah's eyes glittered like the tips of icebergs.

He knew what those eyes saw: a man so afraid of striking out alone he would sacrifice his independence, hand himself over to persons he couldn't be sure were pleased to see him - just to be safe and part of the tribe.

Don't do it, she'd said. *Don't even think of thinking of doing it.*

Too late. Too late. For he had gone and done what she begged him not to, sold the farm the week before. And thinking of his house, its meagre contents, and its only other occupant, what, Tom wondered, would he do about Laddie?

For almost a decade the mongrel had served him, rounding up sheep, alerting him to callers, dozing at the end of his bed, travelling with him on the tractor.

Man's best friend.

What were the chances the two would allow him into their house?

As a the vision of himself tramping the streets of Dublin with not even the dog for company rose up before his eyes, Tom's throat tightened, and he gathered his misery around him like a cloak.

"Tea or coffee?"

The slow advance of a railway employee pushing

a tinkling trolley was welcome relief from his morbid thoughts.

He would order tea when the trolley reached him and try to reason himself into tranquillity. There was no calamity, nothing to dread. A year from now, he would look back and smile. What put him in turmoil was fear of change, and he resolved to overcome that. He would rise like a man to the challenge, take on Dublin, Robbie and Anna.

And so what if their lifestyles differed from his?

They were not without their woes, trying to make out in a fiercely competitive business in a fiercely competitive world.

Understandable they had to look and act the part.

Even he, Tom, knew that success was judged through the trappings of wealth. True, it put the pair on a spending treadmill, but that was where he would step in with his timely financial ballast. Solvent for the first time in his life, was he not ideally placed to help them?

Yes. Help them he would. He had a *duty*.

At the mention of duty, Sarah had heavy-lidded her eyes at him. She took a cloth and viciously swiped at the counter. The clock on her wall chimed the hour. It was the last day of August and the air was heavy with summer. Beyond the open half-door, shadows lengthened into long narrow stripes as the sun dipped behind the distant peaks.

Inside, the denizens of the pub crouched over their pints, heads bent in earnest, muttered conversation while the curtains of dusk gently dropped around them.

Behind the bar, Sarah filled a shot glass with whiskey. In the mirror above a row of bottles, her blue eyes lifted and locked with his.

"Now then, Willie."

She passed the glass to one of the locals, took his note, and gave back change. Then, turning to Tom, "Talking of duty," she said, "There's nothing more bracing for the soul than turning your back on it, now and again."

Tom had bridled at her tone.

"Is that why you're selling your grandfather's licence?"

Words he regretted the moment they left him for Sarah became rigid, her pardonable outrage reinforced by the slamming of her till.

Conscious of a lull in conversation and faces

pointing in their direction, Tom felt himself redden.

His scalp tightened.

The gorge of annoyance within him subsided, giving way to dismay and disbelief.

He waited for the hum of the bar to resume before tendering an apology. And only from the sudden broad smile on Sarah's face as she touched a hand to her hair, did he realise that something that hadn't to do with their scrap was going on behind his back.

"Evening, hello."

The familiar voice came without warning.

Tom glanced round to see the tubby little figure striding through the ranks which parted like the Red Sea to allow him through.

"Thank you. Cheers."

It was the estate agent, McAllister, who, with his booming voice, thrown-back head and charcoal suit, had the air of being descended from a long line of well-bred penguins.

"How's it going?"

Although he acknowledged Tom with a brotherly pat on the back, the greeting was meant for Sarah, the alert interest of whose manner Tom found distressing.

"An all-right time to look around?"

And flashing his gums in a way that had Tom itching to knock him down, he bee-lined towards the kitchen with the relaxed bearing of one who belonged.

Don't-do-it. Don't-do-it.

Tom's eyes focused. He turned his wrist and frowned at the time.

Outside the train, the September day was bright and clear.

In the distance, some golden rolls of hay scattered about a stubble field put him in mind of oatcakes slowly baking in the sun.

And thinking of cakes and homemade bread and a meal he'd had at the Killydoon, Tom sat up electrified, his brain illuminated by a sudden flash of insight. But at that moment something touched his forearm. He turned, to find the backpacker leaning towards him, holding out a can of nuts.

"Like to try some, sir?"

Although the grainy aroma of salted peanuts brought water flowing into his mouth, Tom held up a restraining hand.

"No, thanks, son. But tell me -" He pointed to the

young fellow's iPhone. "Can you find information on a thing like that?"

The youth set down his can of nuts. "What did you want to know?"

Ten minutes later, Tom, for the first time in his life, held an iPhone to his ear.

He slewed his body towards the window, seeing nothing but the little pub, its white walls splashed by the rich yellows of nasturtiums, smoke from its chimney looping sluggishly skywards, pots of geraniums on the two front sills.

"Hello? It's me. I'm on the train."

Tom winced at the absurdity of such an opening gambit which he'd heard expressed on train trips without number.

"Tell me -" He cleared his throat. "You haven't

transferred your licence yet?"

Silence.

He waited with a sick kind of longing that caused his limbs to tremble, his eyes to blur. And when, at last, the low sweet voice husked in his ear, "No, not yet," his heart began to kick in his chest.

"Listen, girl. I know the market price for a licence. I just found out from - the internet. Yes, you heard me, the internet. And the thing is -" Tom worked on controlling his pounding pulse. "I can afford it myself. The licence, I mean."

Thud. Thud.

"And before you ask what's going on, I'm not going back down South. No. What I need is occupation. And I'm thinking in terms of the Killydoon. We could work it together, yourself and myself - two on a raft being better than one."

Tom looked round, shocked to find he had an audience.

And not just the backpacker who gave his best show of inspecting a map, but a trio of women across the aisle who studied him with suspiciously bland expressions before turning away polite eyes.

He had a duty to end the call, and return the phone to his benefactor.

But what the hell, he thought, suddenly possessed by the demon Rebellion.

It was bracing, was it not, to sometimes turn your back on duty?

And so, with a feeling of weightlessness, he powered on, his mind's eye on Sarah, his bodily eye on the map his brand new friend was trying to fold.

But presently, he trailed off into silence, for Sarah had made a sound people who didn't know her might take to be a snort, and Tom's expression when at length she found her voice, ran the whole proverbial gamut from hope to anxiety to alarm to relief and presently back to hope again.

"Thanks, lad," he said some moments later as, with a bobbing Adam's Apple, he handed back the iPhone. "I've one last request before I stand ye a cup of tea. Could ye write down the name o' that gadget. I've a mind to buy one for someone I know."

The Sub-Postmistress

"*Can you spare me a minute?*"

It was all he had to say and had been meaning to say it for at least a year but somehow he could never choke the words out. Not because of the addressee - a woman with a tendency to raise an eyebrow whenever she would see him, and whose hair was the colour of autumn leaves and whose eyes were widely spaced and, well -

No.

The reason he couldn't get the words out was not fear and awe of Anne Marie Delaney but the stutter of which he was deeply ashamed. True, he mostly tripped up on words that began with P or B, but by some terrible quirk of fate his surname was Branigan and his first name Patrick so that even to introduce himself was out of the question.

Add to that that he hailed from the parish of Ballinboro - or more accurately the hinterland beyond it - and you had the makings of a comedy show.

Paddy Branigan of Ballinboro took a long time to say and had occasioned considerable mirth at school bringing out the fascist in some of the townies.

"Know what, Pa? They'd *love* you in RTE. Newsreader like, you know?"

And they'd fall about, mock-punching him on the shoulder while suggesting other occupations he might like to consider - Game Show Host, DJ, roving reporter, or BBC presenter.

But if the school yard was a place of torment he could not in all honesty complain about his teachers. Conscious he had lost his mother at a tender age, they would wait for him with an air of weary patience to say whatever it was he wanted to say, then enjoin him to "slacken the reins".

"Let you try and relax the words will flow."

But Brother Paschal who taught him English, and whose name Paddy would do anything not to have to utter, would sometimes shake his head in despair.

"How you'll cope at interviews I shudder to imagine. Now once again, slowly: *The St Patrick's Day parade paused by Brooklyn Bridge.*"

But although he shrank from this and other violations committed upon him, there was one area in which he shone: he had a singing voice the power and emotion of which would silence even his tormentors, and which resulted in exhortations to sing not just in choirs and school operettas, but at weddings in Ballinboro and the townlands beyond - all of which boosted his confidence and put some money in his pocket.

But there was no future in singing, as Paddy's father was wont to lament. He was to buckle down to study or else come back and work the farm.

After the Leaving Cert, Paddy sought the services of a speech therapist recommended by Dr Whelan, the retired GP who had tended his mother. With time, he showed signs of improvement. But when it came to interviews his heart would rattle like a pea in a can, and the more he would try to relax the more his neck muscles would tense, and he would squirm before his interviewers who, waiting for him to trawl up the elusive words, seemed more embarrassed than he was.

And of course he never got the job.

Nor any of the jobs his educators had suggested - Bank, Garda Siochana, Civil Service, CIE.

Nothing for it but to turn to the farm.

And here he would remain, thought Paddy, deep in the bogs of Allen until Death the Deliverer paid him a visit.

And oh God, oh God, was it not the worst of times, and yet the best of times? Bad, in that five years on Paddy found himself alone, his father having died of what the hospital declared was an aortic aneurysm. Good, in that the country by now had seemed to emerge. A phenomenon brought on by a mishmash of things - a well-educated young workforce, low costs, telecommunications, the lowest corporation tax in the EU, and a sophisticated agricultural sector. All barely registered by the grieving Paddy.

What he did however notice was the slow return of emigrants - one in particular.

Paddy was not yet twenty-five when first he noticed Anne Marie Delaney. She had come to the village of Drish to the shop her aunt had left her. It was an old world grocery known to the locals as Barrett's and which functioned also as a sub-post office. An unlikely setting for a goddess.

Rumour had it she had worked in London for the BBC. In what capacity no one seemed to know. In her spare time she trod the boards by taking part in amateur theatre productions, and it was this which had excited Paddy's interest and given him an idea.

But how to get the idea across? How to even reach her?

Paddy wasn't sure if it was imagination or not, but of late the Barrett emporium seemed more like a barber's than a grocer's. All those males hanging about patiently waiting for Anne Marie to serve them. And the curious thing was the drabness of the shop which was inversely proportional to the splendour of its owner. With its creaking floorboards, rickety shelves and great wooden counters it looked like nothing so much as a stage set for a John B Keane play. And yet, despite this - and the supermarket down the road - business could not have been brisker.

It had to do, of course, with its proprietor. The siren, thought Paddy. Luring them in with those eyes of hers.

And yet, if Paddy were honest, her behaviour was beyond reproach, for she had, by a system of widening those eyes and holding herself aloof, warded off familiarity on the part of the more persistent males - people Paddy knew by sight.

And not just brash young hoods who would go to any extreme to shame a smile from her, but married men who came into the shop and asked for products she didn't stock.

Unworthy behaviour, considered Paddy, who wouldn't dare look up at a queen.

But now. Now, because of something that struck him - something that could change the course of his life and that of others in Ballinboro - he would need to get to her. To communicate. Ought he to write to her then seeing as how he couldn't speak? But - *no*. Paddy couldn't bring himself to write.

Instead, he took to calling to the shop a little oftener in the week and early in the mornings.

But each time he tried to speak, his jaw would tighten and his tongue would cleave to the roof of his mouth, for Anne Marie would gaze at him with something that might have been a smile but could equally be a sneer. And off he would take with his purchases having acknowledged her thanks with a curt little nod.

But he ought not to be so defeatist, he later chided himself. Why not commit his plan to paper, striking out all P's and B's, memorise it, go down to the shop and recite it? No need to state his name, just refer to himself as her neighbour?

All over June and July Paddy prevaricated. But finally the day did come when he took up the pen. And having written what he intended to say, he posed before the bathroom mirror.

"Morning, Miss Delaney."

He smiled at his reflection, pleased at least he was tall and trim. Then, as he approached an imaginary counter, he let rip with his piece, inflating his chest, swinging a little from side to side on the fulcrum of his feet, rounding his vowels while talking in a crisp and sonorous voice - in short, behaving like a confident self-possessed man of the world.

It was the first day of August when he set off in his battered red Datsun and drew up around the corner from the sub-post office. With his heart kicking against his ribs, he entered the shop, waited for a customer to leave before clearing his throat and turning the full intensity of his stare on Anne Marie Delaney.

But gazing into her eyes, seeing that hovering smile, he felt a renewal of his old confusion. His tongue stiffened so as to prevent any utterance, and he became the same insecure figure he had been during those long tormenting years at school. And Christ, he thought, if he could only sit at a piano, close his eyes, and warble out his message.

He grabbed a breath, for it was now or never.

"I'm...your neighbour, Ms Delaney."

His words came haltingly, but not the ones he'd been rehearsing. And there was no inflating of his chest, swinging from side to side, rounding of vowels or deepening of voice.

"B-Branigan's the name and I understand you're Miss B-Barrett's niece and have some experience of theatre work. I have a p-pro...idea might be of interest to you and that is the setting up-pup-pup of a society."

Silence.

"A musical society," he carried on despite that his limbs were shaking and his mouth was opening and closing like a dying fish. "Or failing that an amateur theatre. Thing is, I'm interested in singing myself, and I'm sure we'd not have difficulty in rounding - uh - finding young folks or digging out musicians. If you hap hap happen to have any interest."

Paddy's palms ran with sweat for yet more silence followed on this. Into it came a ripe resounding voice. The voice of authority.

"My dear Miss Delaney, you must close up shop and come into the sun."

And Paddy knew he might as well go, for here was the male counterpart of Anne Marie, someone who had sparked among the women (and not just those of marriageable age) the same noise and clamour the sub-postmistress had sparked among the men. Smooth, refined, urbane, stood Dr Whelan's replacement, Aubrey Goodwin, whose exits and entrances had a theatrical quality which so completely fitted his elegant figure and cropped fair hair that he gave Paddy always the impression of being less a doctor than an actor playing that part.

Just the kind of humbug he would want for his theatre, and to blazes with him, thought Paddy as, with a poisonous glance in Anne Marie's direction, he stormed volcanically out of the shop.

That afternoon found Paddy in Dublin - hardly knowing how he got there.

Having made enquiries about a passport, he shopped in unfamiliar streets, picking up a suitcase and an assortment of clothes. For he'd made up his mind he would sell the farm and move abroad.

By now it was close on six and Paddy's stomach rumbled with hunger. A meal in a restaurant on Stephen's Green had the effect of increasing his woes for he was the only diner who sat alone. Nor did it help that under the supercilious gaze of the waiter who handed him the wine list, he felt his face go hot and cold. He tried to relax but found it impossible.

Everything was entering his brain like a confused and heated dream: the dissolution of his farm, estate agents to-ing and fro-ing, goodbyes to friends, the roar of Melbourne, London, or New York City or wherever it was he was going to go, winters, being alone in a high rise apartment and - worse than any of this - being interviewed for jobs.

With a hollow sensation in the pit of his stomach, Paddy poked at his food. Steak au poivre, he thought disgustedly. Why not steak with pepper? And as for gratin potatoes. Paddy heaved a weary sigh. He set down his fork and pushed his plate away for suddenly it was all too much.

The aroma of garlic, the piped music, the chatter in the room, the clink of china, all seemed at one moment close and at the next far away and wholly unreal. The world hummed strangely about his ears and everything combined to produce in him a mysterious state of stupefaction.

He yearned suddenly for the outdoors, cool air, rolling meadows, grazing cattle, *peace*.

Unbidden, his thoughts shifted to Anne Marie Delaney and that strange unnatural smile she had bent on him in the moment after he'd left off speaking and before Goodwin had made his appearance. Better never to have come across her, for now, the full meaning of his little speech was filtering piecemeal into his mind, ripping him asunder as its delayed action brought wave after wave of scorching pain.

The truth was that he was in love with the girl and had been so from the first moment he laid eyes on her. All that talk of amateur dramatics and musical societies was him making overtures and nothing else. But yes, thought Paddy, as he loosened his tie and called for his bill. He would man up now, sell the farm and head for New York.

It was close on nine when he left the restaurant, and twilight by the time he swung through his gates. He killed the engine at the front of the house, got out and slammed the door. At first, he didn't see her because she was sitting on the doorstep in an attitude of waiting and he'd been distracted by the barking of the collie.

She stood as he approached. And, fool that he was, all he could do was stare.

She smiled, and her teeth in the gloaming were snowy. He had a notion she was furtively looking him up and down.

"Hello."

She smiled a second time, then in a bell-like voice that set his pulse rate soaring, "You asked me a question," she said, "but didn't wait for an answer. And as I don't have a car and you didn't leave a number I was forced to walk all the way here just to let you know that...that I think a musical society in Ballinboro is not a bad idea."

Anne Marie Delaney said other things that had to do with musicians and a hall they might use that was half-way between Drish and Ballinboro, but suddenly her voice seemed to wobble. And when, after coughing into her fist, she added, "I have heard it said you yourself have a splendid voice," Paddy felt a glow expanding around his heart.

He opened his mouth to speak but no words came.

And as he carried on staring, Anne-Marie took a sideways step and seemed as if about to leave.

"Don't," Paddy came forward. "P-Please, don't go." He reddened, realising with amazement he was gripping her wrist. "Thing is, seeing you here sort of robbed me of speech, b-b-but...a mug of tea might loosen my tongue."

Would You Help Me Out, Mary

Every Christmas Eve
Despite the ice and frost and snow
A roaring fight goes on
In a little house I know

Mary, where are you?
Have you seen my cap?
Don't you know I'm going frantic
For I've gone and lost me map

Where's them bleddy socks
You've been knitting half the year?
Are you certain that you've dried out
Me thermal underwear?

Would you ferret out me water jar
And go and fill it up.
Here's some Paddy for me cocoa
Pour in a decent sup.

Darn. Me boots is full a mildew
This is going on for years
No matter how I rant
She'll park them underneath the stairs.

Oh for God's sake put the kettle down
And help me don me coat.
Not the bleedin' black one -
Me RED one, silly goat.

I would need a helicopter
For I'm pushing on in years
By the time I'm sorted out
I have Mary left in tears.

I'm wrecked before I'm started
Yet I fill me sleigh because
The wife is Mary Christmas
And I am Santa Claus.

You Are Dead

"Would you ever sit down? You are making us nervous."

Thus spoke his wife in the presence of six companions who, seated around the table, managed to look everywhere except at him. He excused her on the grounds that with eight units of Merlot inside her, unwisely consumed in the lunch hour, she was speaking with more than her usual peremptoriness.

"What," she asked, "are you looking for?"

Scott Hunter stood frozen as in a photograph, hands deep in the pockets of his ski pants. Talk around him dribbled and ceased and he realised with a rush of anger that Laura's carrying voice could not have failed to reach every ear in the room.

"Hel-*low*?"

"Phone." Scott cleared his throat and tried to inject a note of casualness in his voice as he carried on with his futile fumblings. "I can't seem to find it."

"Sure you brought it with you?" came the mild enquiry from the long lean figure on Laura's left. Alex Barlow, head of a law firm, was a fatherly type with a dominant kind of face seen in those in the habit of command. Sensing a squall and anxious to quell it, he looked up at Scott with an expression of settled benevolence, while at the same time clamping a hand over Laura's wrist. "Don't recall seeing it myself."

But before Scott could answer, Laura was back.

"I thought you kept it in that," Here she paused for an instant and spoke the next three words with unnecessary distinctness as though to parody them, "bag of yours?"

At the mention of which Scott's hands mechanically went to his waistline.

His bum bag. *Where was it*?

"I suppose you'll tell me that's gone too?"

At this, Scott ground his teeth and tried to force his brain to contrive some devastating reply, a rebuke swift and bitter that would scorch itself into Laura's mind and silence her for the rest of the trip. But to engage in verbal sparring was not alone unseemly but foreign to his nature. Better the graciousness of giving in to the winning of sterile battles.

And so, with deliberate nonchalance he hunkered down and burrowed in the backpack he had stowed beneath the table. After which he turned to his ski jacket which was draped across the back of his chair. By which time, the rumble of conversation had resumed, and the blush of which he was so mortally ashamed, had abated.

"Here, Laura, shout out the number and I'll ring it."

Scott glanced up at the camel face of Henry Moorhead seated next to him.

A barrister and distant relative of Laura's late husband, he had a calm and easy disposition, the kind of courtly charm Scott imagined would go down well in the witness box. But beneath his open geniality of manner, his deep set eyes were examining and alert, and Scott had the uncomfortable feeling that since his marriage to Laura - older than him by a lustrum - he had been the subject of much discussion not alone in the Moorhead household but in the Law Society bars.

"Uh, oh. Gone to voicemail."

Scott's knees cracked as he rose and resumed his place at the end of the table. And whereas it gratified him that the others were showing interest - *you'll find you didn't bring it...why can't we wear them like watches?.. anyone thought to talk to Corey?* - across from him, his wife was staring with an expressionless face.

To damp down the fury that that stare of hers so often inspired, Scott looked away to the window thus presenting her with a chilly profile. Outside, where freedom lay, skiers and their guides were coming and going. On the restaurant deck, waiters flitted among the tables. Beyond in the slush, some youngsters engaged in horseplay. Above them, the lowering clouds had taken on a supernatural glow. It had started to snow.

All this Scott saw but didn't register. For his pulse was thudding in his ears as he tried to retrace his steps.

Drag lift.

Before that, the Yellow Valley run.

Before that again, the Misty Mountain Inn three, maybe four, stations back.

Elevenses.

Barlow ordering coffees.

The ladies claiming a booth.

Henry and himself locating Guys.

End stall. Shucking off his backpack, scrabbling for a Valium, washing it down with port from his flask, waiting for his pulse rate to settle following on his shameful ordeal.

Had he taken off his bum bag then?

"Wouldn't bother if I were you. You're not going to find it. Are they, Scott?"

Scott half-slewed around, realising that Laura was

asking him a question. He saw to his consternation that the others were toiling on his behalf - lifting napkins, sliding dishes this way and that, pushing back chairs to peep beneath the table.

Laura alone sat sphinx-like, staring at him in eloquent silence.

He had the wildest urge to lean across the table, seize the water jug and chuck its contents into her face.

But he checked the impulse, and with bitter shame acknowledged that from her point of view there was some justification for her present anger. He was not enjoying himself and taking little pains to hide the fact. For although the others - Barlow and his colleague Claire, Henry Moorhead and his wife Innes, Eric Selby and his partner Clive - had been courteous, kind, and as helpful as one can possibly be on a trip that is less a holiday than a test of endurance - nevertheless an unhappy sense of exclusion had taken hold of him.

He didn't know the others well, for each with the exception of Claire who had come on the scene only recently, were intimates of Laura's and notches above him on the social scale. This despite his medical degree.

To add to his woes, he barely knew which end of a

ski pole was the business end. In fact, despite a school trip in the distant past, and a lesson or two since meeting Laura, he had barely advanced beyond the nursery slope.

And here he now was on the side of Mount Alyeska, the most awesome of Alaskan mountains with - as the brochure declared - the highest percentage of advanced runs compared to any other resort in Canada or North America. The section for the novice is where he ought to have stayed. Not being fit, he had incurred Laura's wrath by lagging behind and forcing the others to loiter.

But worse than any of this had been a weakness he had tried to conceal but was forced that morning to own up to: uneasiness with heights. Two hours earlier, he had not very manfully shown symptoms of panic when their chair lift stalled more than half-way up a vertiginous incline. Glimpses of rock beneath them had not just twisted his bowels but made his sight seem to come and go and the palms of his hands to run with sweat.

"Don't," he had cried, as Laura twisted round to talk to someone on the chair behind.

"Don't what?"

"Stay still, would you."

`What?` Laura pulled down her goggles as though

the better to examine him. Then in that pukka voice of hers, "*Hyper*ventilating? My dear doctor."

And as he sat there, suspended above a ravine, the sweat chilling on his body, a murderous thought stole into his mind. He would lift the bar from above their laps, throw himself down, taking Laura with him.

But shortly after, the engines up the mountain gave out a rumble. The lift jittered. They were on their way.

"Take it, nothing of value in the bag?"

Scott stirred, then turned to the voice.

Eric Selby, two down from Laura, was gazing at him reflectively while tapping a fingernail against his empty glass. A hedge fund trader and gay rights activist, he was seated across from the man he referred to as his husband. Although amused at first on hearing this, Scott couldn't help reflecting that the pair at least were open, their love for each other unabashed and irrefutable - more than could be said for others around the table.

"Apart from the iPhone, I mean?"

"Nothing I couldn't live without."

Scott shifted in his chair and cursed the colour that rose to his cheeks. It had nothing to do with Selby but the figure beside him at the end of the table.

Claire Byers was eating the last of her pudding while hearing out the woman seated across from her. Innes Moorhead, the garrulous wife of Henry, was an American whose low monotonous voice droned on in the background like an annoying bee. Slowly, while Innes was soaring, Claire turned her head and looked along the table. Her eyes lifted and locked with his.

Flustered, Scott reached for the jug and slopped some water into his tumbler.

Laura said something.

Scott nodded gravely.

She said something else, but under the pretext of chasing an itch at the nape of his neck, he glanced again in Claire's direction. It was a sidelong glance, fleeting but intense. He saw that she was leaning forward in her chair, idly toying with her spoon, while shaking her head in patient amused reproof at whatever Innes was saying now.

With her downcast eyes, the delicate line of her brow and nose, the gentle curve of her chin and throat, she might have been carved by some adoring artisan out of a lump of ivory. Who really was she, this thirty-something para-solicitor? What was her relationship with Alex Barlow? Were they colleagues or something more?

"Lie to me, your credits cards are not in that bag?"

Scott brought the tumbler to his lips and over the rim studied his wife as though for the first time, which, in a way, it was. A Wagnerian prima donna of the landowning classes. Hair going grey at the temples. Reading glasses atop her head, their hard black frames suggesting qualities in their owner that would not be easy to live with - vigilance, tenacity, reluctance to ever lay aside armour.

And oh, Sweet Lord, that he whose nature was accepting and inoffensive, should have taken up with such a virago, married her for all the wrong reasons, was of enduring shame to him, and something he would have to answer for at the last bloody trump.

How *how* had it ever come about?

With a sigh that was almost a sob, he let his mind slip back to the Eve of Christmas Eve four winters earlier. The tall majestic figure irrupting into his surgery, ignoring the chair he is holding out and, with tears in her voice, enumerating the symptoms afflicting her since leukaemia took her husband away - apathy, weight gain, insomnia, humming in her ears.

"Is there anything you can do, Dr Hunter?"

He never knew how it came about. One minute she

is swaying before him, the next she is in his arms, sobbing on his shoulder.

He has no idea what to do.

But in the nano-second between raising a hand and touching it to her shoulder, enormous forces seem to be closing in on him, hurling him in opposite directions - forward to a new life, or backwards to Sarah, the girlfriend he no longer loved.

"I will take care of you."

And that had been the start. No formal declaration, no dropping like a stone into love, no purposely built-up scene, no fuss.

I will take care of you.

Had he meant it? Or had some inner voice whispered, *An easy life. You need never work so hard again*?

"I said credit cards. Are they in that bag or not?"

Scott set down his tumbler, uneasily alert to the sudden lull around the table. "You know very well they're with our passports in the safe."

"And what about money?"

Forget it, Laura. You're dead. I am going to leave you.

Aloud he said, "Thirty dollars at the very most."

Laura raised her chin and slowly lowered it as though that much at least had been cleared. But she hadn't finished yet.

"And so, how shall you fare for the rest of the day?"

"Without money, you mean?"

Laura didn't answer. Just sat there, gazing down the length of her nose, the lenses of her glasses glittering at him like a second pair of eyes. Suddenly she snorted, a mocking appreciation of the blank look on his face.

"Not money. No. Your other more important... *goods*. Things no skier should be without."

And she began with a sidelong glance at the others to slowly itemise them, counting them out on her fingers.

"A whistle. A compass. A slab of Marks and Spencer's chocolate. Dutch courage in the shape of *Valium* - "

Scott listened with a smile on his lips, feigning an equanimity he hoped deceived the others.

"... not forgetting the flask of port."

"Well, I can tell you," said Eric Selby in his deep contralto, "without a Valium 5 inside me, I wouldn't as much as look towards an airport."

"Lip balm," carried on Laura, ignoring the interruption. "Sunblock. And - what? - oh yes, a folded balaclava. Darling - "

Abruptly, she leaned across the table, smiling sweetly, cheek raised as though inviting Scott to kiss her.

"Do you know who you really are?" A beat. "Scott striking out for the Antarctic."

A giggle from somewhere behind.

Chuckles from round the table.

And in all that theatre of grinning faces, magnified by Scott's humiliation into the vastness of a
stadium there was one face that didn't smile: Claire's. Sitting upright in her chair, forearms on the table, she gazed at Laura with a kind of cold contempt.

Paralysed with embarrassment, Scott's blood rose slowly.

He was angry with Laura, hurt, outraged, and now inflexibly confirmed in his intention to leave her. And whereas the temptation to leap up and grab her by the throat was overwhelming, he had no intention of letting her see how much her words had stung him.

Wincing, he sank back into his chair and with mock severity, "Bad girl," he said. "No more plonk for the rest of the day."

"No more skiing either," said a voice that was hitherto silent.

It was Selby's lover, Clive, a towheaded man whose considerable good looks were cosmetically aided. He'd raised his head from his text messaging to stare morosely out the window where flurries of snowflakes were spiralling down from the snow-laden sky. He was about to say something else when, "Okay, you guys," came the deep Canadian drawl from somewhere behind him. "Gather round. Good news, bad news."

All eyes turned on Corey, their effusive guide, who was sidling between the tables, snow melting on his hair, ski boots loosened, a Bluetooth jammed in his ear.

"You were on about a fanny pack?" His gaze skittered around the table before coming to rest on Claire.

Claire?

Scott felt a curious tremor in the region of his heart.

Was he to believe that the lovely creature had spoken to their guide - on his behalf?

"Just now I called the Misty Mountain Inn? Incredibly, they have it. Whoever lost it left it in the john? You, sir?" he spun around when Scott theatrically cleared his throat "Well, now, let me tell you - you are one lucky camper. If I was you I'd bomb down now and ask for Jake."

"And the bad news?"

The ever cool Henry was a model of composure as he pushed back his chair and got to his feet. Early in the week he had referred to the Canadian - who had treated them all with an exasperating lack of deference - as a condescending ski bum with an I.Q. lower than his age. What irritated him even more was the young man's

mode of speech - everything he had to say curling upwards into an interrogation at the end - an American import he'd had to put up with even at home. Now he was gazing at Corey as Joseph the Carpenter had gazed on his Son - in pained anticipation of what was coming next.

"Snow like you never saw before?" was Corey's forecast. "Okay, it's stopping now, but give it an hour and we're talking whiteout?"

"Very good. And so what is the plan?"

"Just about time for one more station, then we gotta turn round?"

It was close on two by the time they straggled from

the restaurant. The clouds had split apart to reveal a hairline of screeching blue sky.

In the gleam of the new fallen snow, Scott shook off his feeling of gloom for everything was rounded and softened and Christmas card pretty. The corners of the inn roof were gentle and even, and where a sudden shaft of sunlight caught a slope of unbroken snow, a million diamond facets dazzled the eye.

For a moment he stood there, thinking of nothing.

So tired did he feel, it seemed impossible to uproot his gaze from any object on which it alighted. Ahead of him, Eric Selby clambered down towards the rank of skis, his feet crunching with muffled squeaks across the rounded sequence of the snow. With an effort, Scott summoned his flagging strength and was about to follow in the other's footsteps when he felt a gentle tap on his shoulder.

He looked around and saw Claire drawing a pole strap over her wrist.

A wisp of her hair escaped the confinement of her cap which was pulled down low over her ears.

"Hi."

"Claire."

Examining her at close quarters for the first time, he saw that her skin was lightly tanned and unblemished, her mouth like a piece of delicious fruit, her beautifully spaced eyes the colour of speedwell.

Suddenly, despairingly, he sought for something to say that would even faintly express his feelings for her. A remark which might make light of Laura's behaviour, reveal his plans to leave her and - dare he hope? - open up the future. For something nameless, he felt sure, was going on between them, some unspoken yet palpable sexual tension.

But, so help him, his heart hammered, his throat constricted, and he found himself gulping out the first banal words that came into his head.

"Good of you to put a word in with Corey. I... wouldn't have thought to ask him."

This Claire dismissed with a wave of her ski pole.

She considered him a moment, the corners of her mouth turning up.

"You know, Scott, you don't have to ski every day. Not saying you're not enjoying the challenge, but -"

She wrinkled her nose.

"There's all Girdwood to be explored, you know.

The glacier tubing place, for instance - have you seen it? I imagine it's a lot of fun. Even better than that, dog sledding. We're going tomorrow, Innes and myself, if you'd care to join us?"

It was all she got to say for Alex Barlow was bearing down on them with a set face, skis over his shoulders, poles beneath his arm.

"Tell you what, Scott. You, Laura and I will head on down and get your bag. I know you know where the lodge is, but I've been here before and know the terrain. And you sweet girl - " He beamed at Claire. "Must hurry along. The gang are waiting. Tell Laura to get a move on, would you?"

The clouds had closed over by the time Laura emerged from the restaurant, pulling up the zip of her burgundy snowsuit. Brushing past Scott, she found her skis, snapped her boots into the bindings, grabbed her poles and declared herself ready.

"All right, then. Goggles on, everyone."

With goofy goodwill, Barlow led the procession, coasting along for a moment, stopping to check that all was in order before pointing his skis straight downhill.

Laura followed.

Scott brought up the rear.

"Now, Scott. All you have to do is stick close to Laura. And you, Laura, follow me."

He took off.

With the glow of Claire's invitation still warming him rosily, Scott barely registered the drop in temperature or the snowflakes sifting through the air. After days of clouded apathy, he found he could ski after all. And ski with confidence. Almost with poise.

It was like awakening to a new life wherein he discovered himself possessed of talent, aptitude, power. The slope became suddenly transfigured, and he dropped down the mountainside conscious only of the clear, clean snow coming alive under his skis.

"Hiya, mister."

"Hello, there."

A smile spreading over his face, Scott raised a pole to the snake-like convoy of children who, led by a giant in a luminous snowsuit, whipped down the slope with a speed and grace he took time out to envy, rounded a bend and disappeared.

Scott carried on, feeling two hundred percent alive.

Children, he mused.

A child.

Was it too much to hope for? True, a family was something he and Laura had never discussed. But now. Maybe now -

Gathering momentum, he arrived at the crest of a sharpish incline. Here he paused to catch his breath.

In the valley below was Laura, who, coming onto an incline, tucked her poles under her arm and went into a racer's crouch. Arriving at the top, she straightened, slammed her skis to the left and launched herself up into the air. Her skis hit the snow and she brought herself up with practised ease before plummeting downwards again. Then, as though remembering him, she cut her skis to the side, came to a stop, and turned to look up the slope.

Scott skated downwards, swerving in time to avoid a snowboarder coming in from a different run, then zipping over the ground, he hit the slope at full speed. Skis slicing through the air, he leaned forward to keep his balance for landing, and surprised himself by staying upright.

"You idiot," was Laura's comment on what Scott had considered a notable performance.

If she was angry earlier she was fuming now.

Scott stared at her bemused, his breath ragged in his

throat.

"Yes?" he asked irritably.

He was tired of this pointless warfare which he suspected she secretly enjoyed, even thrived on. Was it any wonder her husband - a decent sort by all accounts - had been willing to pop his clogs at fifty-one.

"What is it this time?"

Laura pulled down her goggles, never a good sign.

"I have lost him, thanks to you."

"Who - Barlow?"

"No, Scott. The Prince of Wales."

Laura leaned towards him, wiping her goggles, snow furring her ski suit changing its colour from burgundy to rose.

"I don't want to see you here tomorrow," she said, in a low menacing voice. "Okay? You don't like skiing and you can't keep up."

Her long hard stare was followed by a dismissive turn of her head. With a deft movement of her hand she positioned her goggles over her nose, and a moment later was off.

Biting back a retort, Scott followed.

It seemed an endless odyssey of losing her, finding

her, seeing her fitfully through the snow. What, he wondered, had become of Barlow? Did he imagine, the fool, they were still on his heels? Where was that blasted inn? Would they reach it before the blizzard struck? Indeed, if what they were skiing through now was not already a blizzard, then he didn't know what was.

Abruptly, his stomach knotted, for alarm bells were ringing in his head.

They weren't, were they, losing themselves in this crazy snow?

Moving away from things - the thrum of engines, other skiers, gondolas, drag lifts?

Was it nerves made him imagine the course was rougher than it should be and not just rough but perilously steep?

"*Laura*?"

He peered through the snow, realising with horror he could barely see his hand in front of him.

"Laura, where are you?"

He drew up by a fir tree - shocked at finding it where a clear run ought to be - pulled down his goggles and looked around.

The cold was a torment, the snowflakes swirling in

bewildering masses. In a numbed trance he watched them, following them with stinging eyes.

"Laura?" he called again. "We're going the wrong way. *Laura*?"

He left off hollering and was gathering force to shout again when he heard it: a blunt meaty thunk. It was followed by silence then a long low moan that seemed to rise up from the end of a well.

As though taken aback by the thunk, the snowflakes abruptly fell away so that for an insane moment Scott imagined the flakes were not sweeping skywards but that he, and the earth and everything on it, were sinking downwards.

He looked around, appalled to find himself poised atop of what looked like a precipice. Beneath him was a slope so sheer it was all but perpendicular.

No hollow, no plateau.

No clinging roots to grab hold of.

At its base was a scatter of boulders.

And the butts of several trees.

Against the bole of one of them was the curled up figure of Laura.

Silent. Unmoving.

Had she plummeted headlong into that tree?

Might she be dying? Even dead?

Shock held him.

"Laura?" he called. "Laura? I'm coming down."

Only he didn't go down.

Didn't do anything, except lean against the tree at the top of his precipice.

Watching Laura. Waiting.

And long after he gauged that even if alive she could no longer feel the cold, the echo of a thousand voices resounded in his ears, low mutterings, insistent voices, all whispering, chanting, reciting the same expression of grief:

The snow was general...falling faintly through the universe...like the descent of their last end...upon all the living...and the dead.

Chilled to the bone, unsure how long his vigil had been, Scott raised his gloved hands, and touched his thumbs to his little fingers.

The exercise pained but reassured him. He daren't think about his toes.

Squatting, he fumbled in his backpack. Just to open it had been almost beyond his powers. He found the balaclava that used to reside in his bum bag. With aching fingers, he drew it on, and over it his ski cap.

It took much longer to screw off the cap of his bottle of Evian. In the end, he was forced to use his teeth.

He threw back his head and forced himself to drink.

Then, suspending his backpack from a branch of the tree - for they would surely ask for a marker - he picked up his ski poles and inched his way back up the craggy slope, kicking down to form ladders of little ridges.

Although the cold cut through him, and his progress was slow, and all about him was eerie and grey, he felt the sun was in his veins turning everything to gold.

Want a White Nail for Your Coffin?

I'm a businessman, respectable
Smoke thirty fags a day
They harden the old arteries
But I'll have to go *some* way

Time was that I puffed forty
Like my brother, poor old bloke
But I cut them down to twenty
When I heard he'd had a stroke

I'm a mother and a housewife
Smoke fifteen fags a day
But I need them for my nerves
Or I'll wind up being put away.

The kids inhale my nicotine
(Feel bad - it ain't a joke)
I should be saving for their future
But it all goes up in smoke

I'm a plumber - never married
Could not afford to wed
I'm smoking day and night
Once nearly burned myself in bed

I'm stinking like a sewer rat
Or so the girlfriend wails
So to cheer myself I smoke five extra
Wretched coffin nails

I'm a multimillionaire
Cigarettes I never touch
I own tobacco firms, plantations,
Casinos, joints and such

Well thank you all for smoking
Don't you stop or I'll be broke
Forget Big C, heart artery
Believe me, just a joke.

I Will Always Love You

*Leav*ing me? My kidney inside you?

Biography

Mary D'Arcy is a native of Co Westmeath, living in Belfast.   Her work has appeared on stage and in anthologies, newspapers and magazines.   Her comic poems have been broadcast on RTÉ, BBC NI, and once on London Breakfast Television (Why Couldn't I have Been Princess Di?) . Her novel, Tale of Hoffman, was shortlisted for the Sitric `Win a Book Deal` 2004.   In 2006 she was shortlisted for the Brian Moore Award Northern Ireland, and in 2007 for the Stella Artois Pitching Award. She was twice short-listed for the Fish Prize. In 2008 she came second in the Mace & Jones Award (Liverpool), and won the Bill Naughton Short Story Competition October of the same year. In 2009 she was winner of the Molly Keane Memorial Creative Writing Award while in the same year her screenplay, Way To Go, was shortlisted for the Waterford Film Festival.   Her novel, Fall of Eve, was on the Harry Bowling longlist 2010.

Her story, Checking Out was optioned by a Northern Ireland production company.   She has in the meantime been collaborating with Jimmy T. Murakami, the filmmaker and veteran of animation, on a project to be animated in the near future. In March 2011 her play for radio In What I Failed To Do was broadcast on BBC Radio 7.   In April 2012 her monologue Butter Pats and Climbing Roses was performed as part of Dermot Bolger production, Tea Chest and Dreams, at the Axis Theatre, Ballymun, Dublin. In June 2012 she was among the winners of the weekly Ernest Hemmingway Sunday Independent Magazine's 6 word story.

Also by The Fine Line

The Perfect Word: The Fine Line Writing Course

The Perfect Word: The Fine Line Writing Course
Audiobook

The Pocketbook of Prompts: 52 Ideas for a Story

Even Birds Are Chained To The Sky and Other Tales:
The Fine Line Short Story Collection

Bixby's Canine Capers by Chris Hammer

The Fine Line is a publisher and editorial consultancy based in Edinburgh. It provides website content; teaches, advises and edits writers; and publishes work that enthrals its staff. For more information, please visit the website.

www.editorial-consultancy.co.uk

Printed in Great Britain
by Amazon.co.uk, Ltd.,
Marston Gate.